STO

W9-CDW-434

THE CHANGE-CHILD

The
CHANGE-CHILD

Jane Louise Curry

Illustrated by Gareth Floyd

Harcourt, Brace & World, Inc., New York

FIRST EDITION

Library of Congress Catalog Card Number: 69-13772

PRINTED IN THE UNITED STATES OF AMERICA

For Judy and David

THE CHANGE-CHILD

ONE

The pony cart clattered across Pont Neuadd into the sunshine that washed the climbing Welsh valley of Nant-an-Afon. Eilian uncurled herself, brushing the straw with its warm sheep-smell from her shawl and skirts. Once the road and the stream beside it escaped from the narrowest part of the valley between the hanging woods of steep Maes-y-Gaer and the dark slopes opposite, you could see that it was still midafternoon after all. The farmer's pony was old or sore-footed, or both, for the mile and a quarter from the village of Aber had seemed to take an endless time.

The pony slowed his pace even more as Eilian caught a glimpse of the long silver wisp of the Aber Falls off to the right, at the far head of the valley. A silver thread binding up the hill's green tresses, she thought. It would make a poem, that, with a bit of thought. But she was too tired to think it out, and her bad foot hurt fiercely. The pony stopped.

"Are you there yet, child? This is as far as I go."

The farmer moved around to the back of the cart to give

9

Eilian a hand down. Quickly, with a movement as here-and-gone as an adder in the grass, she whipped the blue and scarlet silk scarf from around her foot and into a fold of her skirt. It was so fine a thing that he would be quick to think she had stolen it from some fine lady that morning in Caernarvon.

"I will be managing for myself, Rhodri Huws," she said, refusing his hand.

She hopped nimbly from the back of the cart into the road, putting all of her weight onto the good foot and holding fast to the bed of the cart with one hand.

"No need to snap, ladyship." He shrugged and stood there uncertainly. "So, I didn't wish to bring you with me. But I did. You . . . well, I was at Caernarvon fair, you know, and I heard what old Mary was saying, so it's no wonder I was uneasy. Still, William Price says you're a good child, and as it was him asked me to bring you along from Aber, I've done so. Small thanks I'm to have, it seems."

Eilian flushed. The man had been kind in his reluctant way. Only because he was William Price's friend, to be sure. But kind. She tucked her bundle under her arm.

"I'm sorry. I wasn't meaning to be rude. It's only that I must hurry to be home before nightfall. And I must be off. I do thank you."

Rhodri Huws darted a look toward the long low farmhouse behind them by the bridge. Eilian thought she saw a figure draw back from the door at the dairy end.

"I would drive you the mile up the east valley to your path if the road were in better repair," the farmer said. He looked toward the house again. "Well, my woman will have seen us come. She'll be wanting to hear what price the lambs brought. You know the way to the Bwlch-y-ddeufaen, do you?"

Eilian nodded, drawing away. Why did he keep on? The old woman would come out, and old women had razor tongues and sharp eyes for throwing stones. She hitched up her skirt and her petticoat and moved to go.

"Hold there a moment, child! What have you been doing to your foot? And have you no shoes?"

Farmer Huws pointed to the livid bruise on one small, swollen foot, red and black and blue.

"It will be all right. A horse stepped on it, but not so hard as he might have. It's my lame foot anyway," she said, "so it's no matter. My shoes are in here." She touched the bundle.

"Ah well, if you're sure you've taken no real harm . . ." he said awkwardly. Distressed by the calmness with which the child spoke, he began to wonder if there might not be something in what old Mary and some others said about this odd green-eyed girl with the red-gold hair. A *plentyn-newid*, they said. A changeling. Still and all. . . . He moved along beside her, stopping at the pony's head to take hold of the bridle.

"At the road's end it's the turning to the left. Mind you don't take the green track to the right or you'll be stopping the night up in the hills."

"Yes," said Eilian with a patience she didn't feel. "I've been this road before. Thank you, and good day to you, Rhodri Huws."

She ducked in a half bob-half curtsy and was off. She didn't hurry, for there was a long way yet to go. After a while the valley narrowed again and the trees closed in, crowding close until the air was as chill as it had been on the road below the bridge. But walking is warmer than riding, and the sound of the stream downhill on the right made a good music to step to. Her swollen foot ached a bit, but it was half numbed now, and the going was easier barefoot than in her old shoes. They pinched at the best of times.

12

> "The speckled sun is failing
> On pebbles where waters ring
> In a crystal mountain peal;
> The light grows green, and I sing."

She sang to the tune of the water foaming downhill among the rocks. The stream was full from the spring rains and made a sort of harmony to the song.

The cart track and the trees gave out together. To the right, a green path followed the stream around the foot of a hill, climbing to the upper valley of Nant-an-Afon and the lake far above. To the left, Eilian's path to the Bwlch-y-ddeufaen, the Pass of the Two Stones, began its upward climb. It was the harder way, and Eilian turned aside from it down the sunny bank to the stream. She could spare a minute to bathe her feet. The next mile would be a hard climb, and after that it was another mile and a half along the old Roman way before the Bwlch-y-ddeufaen and the track down to Roe Wen.

The water was as cold as the snows of Snowdon, and Eilian gasped with the shock of its chill on her bare feet. The throbbing half-numbness of the bruise was gone. Or at least she could not feel it for her shivering and delight. With a quaver mastered after a word or two, she sang an old song, the *englyn* about Eryri's snows.

> "Oer yw'r Eira ar Eryri, o'ryw
> Ar awyr i rewi;
> Oer yw 'r ia ar riw 'r ri,
> A'r Eira oer yw 'Ryri."

It was a grand song, all vowels and R's and playing with words.

"Cold the snow on Snowdon's brow,
It makes the air all chill;
For cold, I vow, there is no snow
Like that on Snowdon hill."

Still, there were colder things than snow. There were icicle fingers that could touch and freeze the heart on a fine spring morning at Caernarvon fair. Why had Simon Rastall laughed so when he found that she was Eilian Roberts of Roe Wen? From the moment his cousin had caught hold of her, the day had turned upside down with doubt and confusion.

Eilian had hired out to Janet Price at the Caernarvon fair of the spring before and had proved such a fine hand at the spinning and dying that Mrs. Price almost forgave her for being lame and . . . different. Most of the girls in the county were dark and talkative, and Eilian was their opposite. Once, even, Eilian had overheard old Janet telling her husband William that it gave her "such a turn" to look out of her dairy window on a fine day and see Eilian sitting at her spinning wheel among the apple trees, singing songs Janet had never heard before, the child's golden head bent over the spindle and thread. Eilian had wondered whether the good old woman was relieved or disappointed that the Fair Folk never came to dance the ring around her as they had been known to do in earlier times.

At the fair this morning, Eilian had made her way across the *maes*, the field where girls and lads hired themselves out as laborers and maids, to the *polles*. Mrs. Price had given her several small errands, purchases to make at these stalls, where vendors sold everything from cloves and saffron and raisins or taffeta, moccado, and lace, to soap and pins and whale oil. She slipped between the haberdasher's booth and the *polle* where Catti Williams from Llanaber haggled with old Mary over the price of three tablets of soap. Old Mary had one finger hooked over the edge of the balance at the back so that the soap weighed an even pound against the iron weight on the other tray, and as she caught Eilian's eye on her, she glared a warning. Eilian pretended she hadn't seen. Old Mary and her man and his pony sold sundries up and down the Vale of Conwy, and she had once beaten Eilian with a bunch of willow withies for doing no more than whisper a word of comfort in the pony's ear.

"*Dewines!* Witch!" Mary crossed the fingers of her free hand and shook it at Eilian. "Away with you, or I'll be having the constable over here."

Red-faced, she leaned toward Mrs. Williams and spoke for Eilian to hear.

"Twisted leg, twisted heart! Over in the vale it's said the child is a changeling, and I know it for a fact that once she tried to witch my pony."

Eilian stood, quiet, unmoved. She watched the shifting crowd, counted her pennies, and examined the straw baskets and beehives on the next cart stall. When Mrs. Williams took her soap and went muttering away, Eilian turned to face old Mary.

"A packet of indigo, please, and a pound of the white soap. All soap and no thumb, please," she added maliciously.

"Little sneak!"

Mary spat, but then her eyes met Eilian's calm stare. She hesitated and then reached for the basket of soap, favoring Eilian with an ingratiating but unconvincing smirk. With no one close at hand and the constable nowhere in sight, it might be unwise to refuse the witch-child.

Eilian put the soap and dye in her basket, dropping the pennies in the pan of the scales. A clamor—shouts and laughter and shoving—washed across the field just then, and Eilian followed the general rush toward the roadway, drawn by the sound of a harp and singing.

"It's the Anglesey gentry come over with Sir Richard and Her Ladyship."

"Look you, at that one! He thinks he's a rainbow."

"Which one is Sir Richard, do you know?"

"There. There in the black breeches and doublet. Sober as his father before him."

"Like a crow in a flock of peacocks."

"Hush you. Someone will hear."

Eilian squirmed through the crush of bodies, finding shelter at the front beside a burly, bearded farmer. A large crowd of ladies and gentlemen on fine horses rode at an amble out from Caernarvon, where they had been picnicking on the grassy lawns inside the ruined castle. Riding with Sir Richard and Lady Bulkeley were Sir Richard's brother Edward, Justices Broughton and Leighton and their ladies, and Sir Richard Trevor, the Vice Admiral of North Wales. Behind came the Bulkeleys' chaplain with the harp, then Hugh Hughes, the Queen's Attorney, Sir Edmund Rastall of Cardiganshire, and a number of loud young men on high-spirited horses. Among these last was the young man so like a rainbow. Eilian gaped. She had never seen anything so ridiculously splendid. His black felt hat wore a large, curling cockade of red and white feathers, and his azure cloak was lined with red taffeta and fringed with blue. His doub-

16

let was of stitched canvas, his breeches dark red fringed
with black velvet, and his stockings were of yellow kersey
with a bright blue fringe. His ruff was monstrously wide,
his sword handle decorated with a fat red silk tassel.

"Here, now, who is that yellow-haired birdlet gawping
at?"

"Drato!" Eilian muttered to herself. She schooled her face to its usual distant calmness and turned as if to listen to the priest and his harping.

"Do you suppose, cousin Fabian, that she admires my cloak? Or is it my fine feathers?"

"Here, canary bird! My cousin Simon seeks your compliments upon his taste."

The one named Fabian pulled his horse to the side of the road, crowding the burly farmer and catching Eilian by her hair. As she cried out, he let her go, embarrassed by the quick silence in the crowd.

His cousin was not so shy. He spurred his mount forward, scattering bystanders and catching Eilian between the two horses.

"There, girl, have you ever seen a finer pair of boots? The best Spanish leather, they are. Come, now, was that why you were staring so star-struck? Eh, she's an ugly, peaked little thing, ain't she?"

"Hark you! Mind your purses, dear gentlemen."

It was old Mary, pushing herself forward. She pointed.

"It's a *plentyn-newid*, a nasty shriveled thing. And sly. She'll have your buckles and purses in a wink if you don't take care."

"Change-child," went the whisper through the crowd. "Did someone say cutpurse?"

Young Fabian, much sobered, looked at her curiously but kindly.

"Are you, then?"

"I am no such thing. I am maid to William Price from Aber, and my father is Ifan ap Robert of Roe Wen. I've no need to steal. Now, please, may I go, 'my lord'?"

She turned, addressing this last, defiantly, to the young rainbow.

Simon struck at his prancing, shifting horse and leaned down to take a closer look at her.

"Who'd you say you were daughter to? Ifan Roberts? Of Roe Wen?"

Eilian nodded, suddenly fearful at the sharpness of his scrutiny.

"Then you'll be Eilian."

It was not a question but a statement, heavy with contempt and amusement. He laughed. Eilian shrank away, and the horse started nervously, swinging its head at her. For a moment one heavy, shod foot came down upon her own, and she cried out.

"Mind your horse, Simon," snapped the one called Fabian. He had seen the misstep and the thin, fragile ankle hidden beneath the red petticoat. "Come away," he said. "The others are gone along to watch the football match."

"But I must be bidding my bird farewell! Shall I promise her that when she's mine, she shall live in a cage and have bits of bread to eat? Lucky she is, indeed! Tell your overreaching father that Simon Rastall sends him fond greetings, little bird-bride."

"Simon! You forget yourself, sir!"

The voice was low, quiet, but full of rage. Sir Edmund Rastall rode alongside his son and grasped his horse's bridle, pulling him sharply away.

Fabian, the cousin, hung behind for as long as it took to whip a large square of silk from a slash pocket in his doublet.

"Here, birdlet. Bind up your foot with that."

And they were gone. That was all. Rastall? That was the name some in the crowd had whispered. But who *was* Sir Edmund Rastall, and what had his son to do with her or her father?

Eilian had fled to the stock pens to find Mrs. Price and, in her agitation, told the farmer's wife all of what had happened. She poured the story out, much to Janet Price's amazement, for that good soul had never heard the girl speak such a string of words at once in all the year she'd had her.

"It is a strange thing," she agreed. "Your father couldn't have betrothed you to this young man while you were a babe in the cradle? And not have told you?"

That couldn't be. Not Dad. Not him. Dad was the only one who paid her any mind at all. The only one who stroked her hair and called her fond and silly names. And then, too, the young man had been so fine, and his father a knight. It made no sense. Her father was a poor yeoman, with only a bit of a farm. What should his daughter be doing marrying a son of Sir Edmund Rastall? She hoped it had been some kind of nasty joke, a mean taunting. Bride, indeed!

Eilian worried the whole of the ride back to Aber, and Janet Price fretted with curiosity. When the cart rolled into the Price farmyard on the slopes outside of Aber, it was Janet who suggested that Eilian take a day or two to go home to unravel the mystery. While Eilian bound her shoes and her few bits and pieces into a bundle, William Price went into the road to stop Rhodri Huws as he passed by.

"Rhodri will be taking you as far as Pont Neuadd," said William, lifting her into the cart. "And here, child. Likely there's nothing wrong at home, but if there is and you can't be coming back to us directly, here's your wages for the year past. You've been a good girl."

He unfastened his purse and counted out ten shillings. Eilian tied the coins snugly in a corner of her shawl.

She felt the hard lump that was the money under her hand now. Mam would be pleased with that. She shivered and then started in alarm, suddenly aware of the long shadows that had crept up the valley, washing over the bank where she sat. The sun had slipped behind the trees on the western hills, and when she moved, it seemed the cold of the water had turned her bones to ice. She felt the chill deep under her breastbone. There would be no getting home before nightfall now.

Quickly swinging her feet from the water and gathering up her bundle, she crawled up the grassy bank to the path and pushed herself erect. She walked a few yards like a drunken man and then fell, for the cold had made her leaden feet as disobedient as if they had been asleep. A second time she stumbled and picked herself up, making for the path to the Bwlch. On the hillside above, sunshine still brightened the grass.

"One day," she announced to the deaf hills, loudly, defiantly, "one day when I am a poetess and famous, I shall have a pony all my own, and a servant to set me on it!"

The pinpricks went away, but as the track climbed more steeply, Eilian grew tired. She grudged stopping to rest, for it was hard to keep ahead of the stretching shadows. After crossing the first of the tracks bending down toward Llanfairfechan, she had more level going for a mile, for the way

followed the grass-grown track of the old Roman road from
Caerhûn to Caernarvon. There, however, moving into the
shadow of a hill, she was slowed twice by the crossing of
small streams. Their stones were cruelly hard. Dusk grew in
the grass, and once she came near to treading on a hare.

From above, near the Bwlch, she heard a whistle, a
sound of hoofs, and one sharp bark from a dog. Her keen
ears caught the movement across the hill, and she knew it
was one of the farmers above Roe Wen out to catch his
ponies after their wild wintering on these hillsides below
the mountains. If only it were Rowli Jones and she were
quick enough, she might catch a pony ride down to Roe
Wen.

Her limp worsened as she tried to hurry. The bad foot
didn't hurt, but it was like a dead thing, it was so tired—
making each step only because she swung it forward, pulling
with knee and thigh. Her anger rose in her throat. She
hated her foot, and Rowli Jones—if it was him—whistling
on the darkling hill, and all the grass that grew and hares
that ran, and Simon Rastall, and Mam and Dad. . . . And
then she began to weep, quietly, without a sound, for she
heard the clatter of hoofs on stone, and the slap of a closing
gate, and a snatch of a rousing psalm echoing between the
hills of the pass and fading out of hearing:

"Disgwyliaf o'r mynyddoedd draw
    Lle daw im help wyllysgar;
Yr Arglwydd rydd im gymorth gref,
    Yr hwn wnaeth nef a daear."

When Eilian reached the gate in the stone wall that cut
across the pass, she saw two shadow-ponies moving far be-

low, herded by the dog, followed by a squat cloaked figure on a third pony. They had made a turning above the tree line and the road's steep drop, angling down to one of the high farms. It was not old Rowli after all.

There was no use trying to go farther. The village was a far three miles below, and after a few hundred yards the grassy track became a rutted, stony road. A misstep on the downhill way could be dangerous. Eilian scanned the slopes. No sheep were there, but two pony shapes trotted away from the wall where it bent to cut directly upward. They seemed to be watching her, curious and suspicious. Behind and below, the land was obscured. Here and there beyond the straits and the Lavan Sands a lamp winked on distant Anglesey, and in the sky above the unseen Irish Sea, only a pale grayness lingered.

The ponies' sheltering by the wall decided Eilian, and she passed through the gate, fastening it after her. She was sorry about there being no sheep. Silly as they were, she knew ways to lull them, and a nice warm ewe or two would have made the best of bedfellows. At home in wintertime when the animals came indoors, she always slept among the sheep. The cow, Alis, smelt sweeter, but the sheep were softer.

Finding a good spot in a crook of the wall, she pulled handfuls of grass, lining a sort of nest. The new grass was too short, but here and there she found wisps and clumps of the old grass, pale in the deepening dusk. As she settled down, back to the wall, she undid her bundle. There was a pair of warm hose, and these with the shoes would keep her feet warm. Putting the shoes on was not easy, for her feet were horny from going barefoot, and both were swollen.

But it was done, and with the shawl snug around her head and shoulders and her hands wrapped in the soft silk scarf, she wriggled back against the grassy base of the wall. Perhaps the ponies would come back. If they belonged in the village and were not truly wild, they might come close, even settle down to sleep here.

The shelter held her own warmth about her, but the throbbing had come back to her bruised foot, and she could not sleep. The ponies came closer, moving tentatively. She could hear their falsely casual stops and starts, and laughed silently in the folds of her shawl. She knew that they would be tossing their heads at each other, pretending nonchalance, moving in narrowing arcs toward her nesting place, eaten by curiosity. She laughed aloud, unmindful of the silence and the cold, and heard the ponies pause.

"Now, old Mary would have it that I can speak your tongue, that I can talk with your kind and with the birds and all! Will you be coming to me, then? We can gossip here together, and you can tell me how it feels to run races with the wind. Or shall I sing to you? Yes, that's the way. What will you have? A song of the Fair Folk? My mam thinks they stole her firstborn and left me in her place. Shall I make you a song of that? In what measure? An *englyn unodl union*, perhaps? Oh, harping I know would charm you sooner, but I've no harp, sweet sirs. One day when I am rich, I *shall* have, though." Her high sweet voice rang out:

"Who has seen the likes of this?—no, not I,
    unless a change-child 'tis.
Bathe it in foxglove, ywis.
It will be gone in a trice.

"A hot shovel's better yet—for the fire
will make the change-child fret . . ."

The ponies had stopped their moving when the clear notes first sounded, and when their soft nickers—full of some strange, urgent joy—cut across her song, she faltered and left off.

"That's a bitter ditty, mistress. Surely you've not been bathed in foxglove or thrust in the fire, for here you are, singing and shining?"

Something, someone, touched her hair. The voice was light and teasing. Only a boy, she judged, after the first fright. But no one she knew.

"Who are you so late out on the hills?" she ventured.

A slight, dark figure moved away from the black ribbon of the wall.

"My name is Wesantos—'Gwanwyn' in your tongue. But you may call me Goronwy."

"*Gwanwyn?* But that's no name!"

"Goronwy, then. And you, I remember, once watched sheep here on the hill pastures. You're from Roe Wen, below? And called Eilian?"

Not two in one day! She shrank into her nest.

"How can you know that? I don't know you. And *Gwanwyn* is the springtime, not a name. Where are you from that you know of me?"

"Oh, up yonder."

He waved a shadow-hand toward the hill Drosgyl and the hidden peaks climbing behind it toward Eryri.

"But no one lives up there. Except in the *hafotai*, the summer huts, when the sheep go up."

25

"No mind," he said vaguely. "Tell me about your song. Is it such an evil thing to be a changeling? Why should folk torment them so?"

"Why, everyone must know that! If you torment the *plentyn-newid* enough, the fairies—the Fair Folk, I mean—will come rescue him and give the real child back."

"Ah! And none have come to rescue you, little poetess?"

"I am no changeling!" Eilian flared. "My dad is my own, and my mam, too. Dad says if every babe who fell into a fit or a wasting sickness were a change-child, the Fair Folk would have overrun the country long ago."

"Your father's a wise man, then."

"Yes," she said more calmly. "And he is good to me, you see."

"And do you mind so much that your dear leg has wasted away?"

He said it with such a queer quirkish tone that Eilian laughed despite herself.

"No, not really. It's a good enough foot if you're kind to it. It's only that folk . . ."

"Aye, there's always that," he said.

Eilian could feel him smiling.

"Well, I'll whistle you up a pony," he said, suddenly brusque. "And we'll ride you down the hill home."

TWO

"Is this the turning, then?"

Eilian hesitated. "Yes . . . yes, it is. But how queer it looks."

She loosed her grip on the pony's mane and, leaning forward, stroked his neck reassuringly. The reassurance was more for herself than the solid little pony, who obeyed Goronwy's sign to stand still with the alert docility a good dog shows at a shepherd's whistle.

"Queer? How?"

Eilian looked about her unsurely. The stone wall seemed somehow higher. And . . . yes, the gate was heavier and hung between two pillars of mortared stones. But the great tree beyond the gate was the same yew whose wide-spreading branches had hidden her for so many hours on summer evenings, while she listened to the stream down the hill as it whispered its way through the village and wound away down to the Conwy. Beyond the yew the old cottage of Llwyn Cerddin bulked dimly against the dark hills and sky. It, too, was somehow strange, larger than it should be.

"No, don't get down," said the boy, seeing her hesitation. "I'll unlatch the gate and ride you to the door. I expect

27

your dad's been doing a bit of building, that's all. I've not heard of anyone's leaving the village, or new folk coming in, so you may rest your heart there."

Eilian held her bundle closer and wound the fingers of her one hand in the pony's mane again. Of course. Mam had been harping after Dad for years to mend the tumbledown wall. As the pony stepped briskly down the bit of road to the cottage, Eilian saw the glow of firelight through the uncurtained windows.

"Look there! Are you sure this is Llwyn Cerddin? The windows are glass, and there's more cottage than there should be!"

At the door she saw the IR Dad had carved in the lintel and knew they had come right after all. She slipped from the pony, her tiredness gone in the rush of curiosity. She knocked loudly on the oaken door and called out, for it was bound to be barred against thieves and strangers after nightfall.

"Dad! Mam? It's your Eilian!"

A murmur of exclamations rose behind the heavy door, and there was a sound that might have been a bench knocked over.

"Eilian? It can't be Eilian." She could hear her mother's voice rising sharply in protest. "Have a look out the window before you are unfastening that door, Ifan Roberts."

There was the sound of the heavy bar sliding back, and then her Dad's tall, solid shape stood dark against the fire-glow and candlelight of the warm room.

"Eilian bach! Betty? Anna! It's your sister home from Aber."

Mam's voice cut across Dad's greeting.

"Elizabeth? Angharad! Come away from the door or you'll take a chill from the night air."

Dad folded Eilian in a bearish hug, sweeping her up and across the threshold.

"Pah, it's Eilian who's more likely to take a chill. Why, you're cold to the bone, child! Here, Mam, give way. Let the child sit next the fire."

He bent his head down, moving under the low, blackened oak beam into the great fireplace and set her on the stone bench beside Mam. Mam slipped an arm around her, smoothing back a straggling lock of gold hair with a surprisingly gentle touch.

"Sss. You *are* a sight, poor love. You've not walked all the way from Aber, have you? You'll not be able to hobble for a week, you'll be that stiff in the morning."

Eilian twisted free.

"Gwan—Goronwy! I forgot! We've shut him out, and after he was so kind to me. Dad? He brought me down from the pass on one of his ponies. He'll want warming up, too."

Dad went to the door, opened it, and looked around. He gave a call, and after a few moments and no answer, he barred the door, turning back to the others.

"There's not a soul out there now, girl."

Elizabeth and Angharad, too, had crowded into the warm cavern of the fireplace. Under the rush of their questions and petting, Goronwy was brushed from Eilian's mind.

"Are you stopping at home, sis? Come, do!"

"Say you needn't go back directly."

"You've grass in your hair, did you know?"

Angharad nestled close, giving Eilian a love squeeze, but in a moment she drew away.

"Yuh! You do stink of sheep, Eilian!"

Eilian looked at her curiously. "Beg pardon, mistress! But it's only days since the sheep have gone out on the hills. And today I've been to Caernarvon with a cart full of lambs. Come, why should you mind a warm smell now? You never put on such airs before."

Her mother drew gently away. "The girls don't sleep with the creatures now we've come up a bit in the world."

"Where's Alis, then?"

Eilian looked about her, suddenly aware of the strangeness of the room. The dogs, Spot and Second, dozed on a rush mat near the hearth, but the cow Alis was not in her corner, and no orphan lambs nestled under the table. Every spring-time she could remember, there had been at least one. Instead, there was a clean, fresh scattering of rushes on the floor, and four handsome, sturdy chairs instead of the rude benches that had stood by the table. Mam's loom sat in its old corner, but the colorful woven hangings at the far end of the room, striped in indigo and yellow and scarlet, meant that she'd not had to sell all of her work this year. There were even pewter candlesticks on the table, and a pewter dish and a silver spoon lay among the wooden bowls that held the remains of the evening's meal. A pewter pitcher stood on a worktable in Alis's old corner.

Dad beamed. "You wouldn't know the old place, would you? Your mam's kept me busy all the winter, doing it up."

"I saw the gate, and the windows. It's all so . . . so *fine*."

"Ah, but you missed seeing the dairy. You must have a look first thing in the morning. It's no more than a bit of a room added on t'end of the cottage, but Alis and her daughter take up only a half of it. We'll be able to keep the next two heifer calves she gives us."

Betty sprang up from the hearth and ran across the room. "Look, Eilian. This is the very best of all!"

Seizing the heavy curtains, which were hung by loops from a long pole high across the room's end, she pulled one half aside. Mam and Dad's heavy wooden bed stood in its old place beside the smaller fireplace in the far wall, but it boasted a bright new coverlet. Above it, supported by thick oak beams, Dad had built a plank floor, and on this upper level Eilian could see the ends of two smaller beds.

31

"A loft! Oh, Dad, not even William Price has such a fine crogloft. It's beautiful!"

Mam smiled. "No one in Roe Wen can match your dad working with their hands. But there's more to be done yet. There will be a wall where the hangings are, right up to the ceiling, with a door into what's our room now, and steps up to the loft."

Eilian was excited and bewildered.

"But—all this, the fine things on the table. . . . When I went away, we'd not two shillings to rub together. What's happened? Has Mamgu died and left us a hoard of fairy gold?"

Betty and Anna laughed, but at their mother's glare smothered the giggles in their aprons. Mam was always uncomfortable about the fascination her old mother had for the children. It was not right for a grandmother to fill little ones full of strange tales or hint at magical secrets and other silliness.

"Nonsense. Mamgu is sure to outlive us all. It would be like her," said Mam. "Come to think of it, my girl, it was to earn money you were sent away. Janet Price hasn't turned you off, has she? You've not been thieving from her? Or causing trouble?"

Dad half reached out a hand in protest, but held his tongue.

Eilian's heart turned over heavily, and all the morning's worry came flooding back. Pulling off her shawl, which she did not need in the warm room, she felt for the corner where she had tied the coins.

"Here, Mam. For you."

She poured the ten silver shillings into her mother's palm.

"I'm to go back to the Prices' tomorrow if I may, but

William Price gave me my year's wages, for fear . . . you see, I've not spent even a penny."

Dad frowned. "For fear of what, Eilian bach? You've a worried look about you I don't like, hasn't she, Mam? And how sore your feet must be! Betty, Anna, fetch a basin and some hot water for your Eilian. A good soak will keep the stiffness away."

"And crush a few leaves of Mamgu's herb-whatever-it-is in the water," Mam directed. "Mamgu says the infusion is soothing for blisters and bruises."

Dad gently unfastened Eilian's shoes and eased the hose off while Mam bustled into the bedroom. Anna brought the basin, setting it at Eilian's feet, and Betty unhooked the kettle from over the fire, filling the basin half full and then tempering it a little with cold water from a new pitcher. Anna crumbled a few dried leaves into the water, and a cool fragrance like a meadow in spring filled the room.

Mam came back through the curtains with a clean linen smock and a length of coarse muslin.

"Here, now," she commanded, "off with those dirty, smelly clothes, my girl. Right down to the skin. I'll give you a bit of a wash while you stand in the basin, and then you can slip into Dad's old smock here. Right now you're not fit to sleep in a proper bed. Elizabeth and Angharad shall sleep together for the one night. You shall have Anna's bed." Try as she might, Mam kept slipping back to the comfortable old "Betty" and "Anna," even though she loved the richer sound of "Elizabeth" and "Angharad."

Standing in the warm water, being washed and rubbed by Mam and the girls, Eilian felt the sick, heavy feeling ebb away. When she was dried and dressed again in an under-shift and Dad put his question to her once more, she could

33

close her eyes and tell the whole of the morning's tale without faltering.

"And so I decided to come away home."

Her voice was muffled as Mam pulled a smock down over her head, and when she opened her eyes in the quiet that followed, it was to see an exchange of worried, half-fearful glances.

"What does it mean, Dad?" whispered Betty.

"Will they be taking Plaseirian away from us, Dad?" Anna pulled at his hand.

"No, no, child," he said. "Don't fret yourself."

Mam had gone very still. Her eyes were sharp black specks in a pale, set face.

"Hold your tongue, Angharad." She clapped her hands together. "Elizabeth? Both of you, off to bed! It's past time, and this is no worry of yours. It's no more than some mad prank of Sir Edmund's spoiled brat. Go along with you now, and no whispering."

"Plaseirian? What has Plaseirian to do with it all?" Eilian was bewildered. She shivered under the smock and went to stand nearer the fire. Dad brought a blanket from the bedchamber to wrap about her.

"Here, then," he said, sitting on the fireplace bench and slipping an arm around her shoulders. "You'll need to be warm and snug for such a long story as this is. To tell the truth, the world's a bit upside down since you left us, my girl."

"Ah, don't spin it out so, Ifan," said Mam sourly. "The child will be asleep before you've got to the heart of it. To make a long tale short, Eilian, it's that you are an heiress. Young Rastall must mean to court and wed you to get Plaseirian back for his precious father."

34

"An heiress? But that's daft. Why should he think me one? And what've we to do with Plaseirian?"

Plaseirian was the great house on the largest of the hill farms north toward Conwy. For as long as most of Roe Wen could remember, the house had stood empty while the lands were farmed by a succession of tenants. Few of these tenant farmers had stayed on for more than five or six years because the landlords had always been too grasping, the rents too high. The house itself, even with gaping holes in the slate roof and crumbling plasterwork, was in its old-fashioned way as impressive as Plas Mawr in Conwy, though it had never been so elegant or comfortable.

"Well," said Dad, "it may be that one day Plaseirian will be yours."

Mam nodded. "Aye. Though it would be better if Elizabeth or Angharad were the eldest, for they're far more likely to marry lads fit to manage such a big farm. *And* more likely to keep the place up as it deserves."

Eilian's bewilderment showed in the perplexed quirk of her brows.

"Ponies will wear wings next! Come, you're making no sense, are you? How should the great farm be coming to *us?*" She looked around the snug room. "And how should all this be so fine when Mam has always said we were so poor?"

Mam explained. "Your blessed dad would have been content in a summer hut, and because his father was poor before him, he never thought to raise himself. But now it seems his great-grandmother was the first mistress of Plaseirian, though he never told us a word of that! All this time and we might have been living in a rich house, and him with

35

a great dairy herd and more sheep than any yeoman in the valley."

"Hush you," said Dad, looking uncomfortable. "Eggs may be broken before they're hatched."

Eilian clapped her hands and crowed. Simon Rastall was forgotten.

"But how wonderful! Betty will have all the ribbons she wishes, and Anna her kitten. And, oh! May I have a harp when we are rich, Dada?"

"Hush your teasing." Dad stood and, turning, set her in his place on the seat. Then he paced back and forth in front of the fire.

"It's not good to speak so. Nothing is settled yet, you see. It's all such a muddle with documents and lawsuits and depositions, and the justices and lawyers likely to quibble for years. I begin to doubt they'll ever unravel it. There are times when I wake in the middle of the night to find myself wishing Attorney Llewellyn had never found the letter that began it all."

He went on to explain. "It was when Mr. Llewellyn's father-in-law, Attorney Bennett, died that he found a letter among some old papers; a letter from my great-grandmother Bronwen to an earlier Bennett lawyer. In it, she set down that all her property was to go to her daughter Elizabeth Pugh. That was my grandmother, born Elizabeth Mathews. But then, you see, after the death of her first husband—Elizabeth's father—Bronwen married again. Her second husband was a knight from Cardigan, a Sir James Rastall. It seems he took her away to his home, having rented the Plaseirian lands, and she was never in Caernarvonshire again. When the both of them were dead, Plaseirian went with the other Rastall lands to a nephew, a Rhys

Rastall, father to the Sir Edmund you saw this morning."

"What ever happened to poor Elizabeth?"

"Ah, hum." Dad ran his fingers through his graying curls. "She was only child to Bronwen and David Mathews. An heiress. And there was a neighbor, Emrys Pugh, at Bryn Farm who coveted Plaseirian, and so he stole her away and married her—at which her father disinherited her and willed all he had to Bronwen absolutely."

At the "stole her away," Eilian shrank into her corner by the fire, her alarm checked only by her curiosity.

"It was a spiteful thing her father did," said Dad, "for not long after her mother married Sir James and left the county, Elizabeth's Emrys ran upon hard times. My grandparents lost even Bryn Farm, and old Bronwen never knew of it. But now that I've Bronwen's letter, we can set all right. Mr. Llewellyn thinks the letter may have been mislaid intentionally. Old Bennett had some dealings with Rastall and may have found it worthwhile to keep mum. Not that it's easy. Because it promises to take so long to get a judgment from the Quarter Sessions in Conwy—Rastall refuses to appear, you see. Mr. Llewellyn says I'm to go to Ludlow, where he himself will be drawing up my bill of complaint to the Council of the Marches. They can award us possession of Plaseirian for the time being, he says, for it could be years before the lawyers at Conwy have done with their haggling. Meantime, I've been to the moneylender in Caernarvon to borrow a bit on our expectations."

While he spoke, a dreadful sureness had come upon Eilian. Mam's guess had been only half right. Sir Edmund Rastall meant to steal her away and wed her to that meanmouthed turkey cock of a Simon, all to keep the great house and barns and lands of Plaseirian in his own pocket. She was sure of it.

Mam had taken up her needle and was stitching at a leafy pattern marked on the yoke of a half-finished linen smock.

"Think of it! In a week you'll be off to Ludlow, Ifan. And if all's well, in a month or two I shall be sitting by a fire in Plaseirian's hall, stitching with colored silks instead of coarse linen thread."

"Then may I stay home please and not go back to Janet Price?" Eilian watched her mother fearfully as she asked.

"Don't be daft. There's naught you can do around here that Anna and Betty cannot do in half the time. And Mamgu is coming soon, so we'll be crowded enough. You'll come home when we've gone to the big house and let this one to a tenant. I suppose you may have a room and a proper bed to yourself there, and you shall have to begin learning to be a lady."

Mam did not look up as she spoke and so missed seeing her husband's look of innocent delight in the prospect of riches fade to a frown of concern.

"It's a sad-looking heiress you are, Eilian. What are you thinking?"

She answered:

"Dear yellow birdlet in the wicker cage,
    How came you to be caught?
Beware my lass, trust men not,
For I was stol'n, not bought.

"This morning begins to make more sense," she said. "They mean to steal me away. Don't you see?"

It was a new thought, and Dad did not like it. He left off his pacing and pulled a chair from the table nearer the fire.

"Aye. It could be. I'm not saying it is, but it could be. They wouldn't expect I'd give it you for a dowry in such a case, but Plaseirian would come to you when Mam and I were dead."

"Nonsense." Mam bit off her thread. "She's hardly more than a baby. And so small to be as near thirteen as she is. How could young Rastall hope to marry a lame child?"

Dad shook his head.

"Lameness is little to a greedy man. And as for stealing from the cradle, it does happen. There was Jane Davies only a year ago."

Mam stuck herself with the needle in her agitation.

"No, you're spinning fancies, the both of you. There's nothing in it. And what if there were? Your great-grandfather David Mathews knew the answer to that, Ifan Roberts."

Dad bridled. "Disinherit our Eilian? Is that what you mean, woman? She'd still be wed to that Simon. How am I to undo that?"

He beckoned Eilian to him and gave her so violent a hug that she squeaked. The sound was so comical that they both laughed.

"Oh, stop your precious fooling," Mam snapped. "Many's the girl who'd think herself fortunate to be so wed. A baronet's son is a baronet's son, knave or not. The child would be a lady and go in silks."

"The more fool you," said Dad. "If she didn't bring the promise of Plaseirian with her, she'd not be a lady long. One day word would come from Cardigan that she'd fallen into a consumption or had a bad fall and cracked her head. I've heard that Lloyd Guto of Llanrwst kicked his first wife down the stair when her father held back ten sheep from

39

her dowry. The poor little thing didn't survive it."

"Oh, shut you up! I'll listen to no more of your fantasies. You'll be giving up going to Ludlow next. You've never really cared whether you lived in Plaseirian or a hovel, Ifan Roberts. You'd like nothing better than an excuse to stay here and scrabble at this scrap of land until your hands are as horny as your father's before you."

"There's worse things than having honest calluses, old girl, and don't you forget it."

"Meaning that my father was a thief?" She shrieked. "That's right. Oh, lovely! I knew we should come around to that sooner than later. Why do you suppose that I care you should have a good name and be looked up to? Why should I want my girls to be pretty and fine? You can't *think* what it was like to be no more than six years old and be sent alone in the dark to throw the skins of stolen sheep in the river. When Mamgu begged Dad to take his own risks and not dangle me before the hangman, he beat her. He said they might hang him, but they'd only flog me. Yes, I *want* a soft bed. And taffeta petticoats, and shopkeepers' wives to curtsy to me. What is so sinful in that?"

"Nothing, my girl, nothing." Dad soothed her awkwardly. "And you shall have them, too. But the child must stay at home where I can keep an eye on her. I mislike this Rastall business."

Mam flared again. "And I mislike having the whole of the village reminded I've a queer daughter and a mother queerer yet. Both at once is too much!"

"That'll be enough." Dad's voice was quiet, but it trembled with the slow anger that swelled in him. He pushed the chair back and stood, tall and heavy and red-faced. Eilian had never seen him so angered. Mam gathered up her nee-

40

dlework and edged along the wall toward the bedchamber, half fearful that he might strike her. He never had, but Mamgu said that all husbands came to it in time.

"I meant no harm, Ifan. But we've not beds for the both of them."

"Eilian shall sleep in the dairy with Alis, then."

"Very well." Mam disappeared behind the curtains into the lower bedchamber.

"I shall like that better anyway," whispered Eilian. "Might I sleep in the dairy tonight? I've never slept in a bed. I'm sure I should roll out and tumble off the edge of the loft onto my head!"

Dad turned to her, not hearing at first. Then he mastered himself and managed an absentminded sort of smile as he gave her a gentle push. "Up the ladder with you. In the morning you can sing us a carol about falling out of bed. There's time enough to move in with Alis when Mamgu comes."

He unbarred the door to put Spot and Second out, fastened it again, snuffed out the candles, and watched Eilian make her way up the loft ladder by the dim, warm light of the failing fire. Only after she had stretched out on the cot and heard the leather straps of the bed below groan under Dad's weight did Eilian remember that she'd had no supper. Her stomach creaked in complaint, but she settled down into the soft mattress and tried not to worry about sleeping so high in the air. She was glad Mamgu was coming. Mamgu, who spun stories and called herself Queen of the Red Fairies because of her faded red-gold hair and then laughed. For some reason Eilian remembered her own words—"If you torment the *plentyn-newid* enough, the fairies will come rescue him and give the real child back."

THREE

Days went by quickly, better and worse mixed up together. Mamgu had come. Because of her, today had been best of all.

Eilian wriggled deeper into the straw heaped in the vacant stall and rehearsed to herself all the many things she wanted to tell Mamgu come morning. They were to go mushrooming again, and Mamgu had promised to begin teaching her something about which were good and which were dangerous. Mam hated mushrooms, and Mamgu said that was because once when Mam was a young girl, she had made a soup of the prettiest ones and become desperately sick from their poison.

Mamgu had snickered when she told the tale, covering her mouth with the hem of her rusty black skirt. She had been sitting, herself like a large black mushroom, pale of hands and face and faded hair, in a patch of ferns under an oak tree.

"Here, child, give me a hand up. Hmph, yes. Your mam was green as grass. Heh, there's a piece of wit for you! Green-ignorant and green-ill. She would have it that there were easy rules about mushrooms and toadstools, and it was simply a matter of learning 'em. Hmph!"

Eilian had bent to help the heavy old woman up from her knees. Mamgu's eyes were so dim now that she had to crouch low over each new mushroom, peering, sniffing, touching. As she tugged, her hands under Mamgu's elbow, Eilian's head swam from the musky sweetness that rose from the folds of the ancient black dress.

"It's like your poetry, child. It's more than an art. It's a gift." She darted a sideward glance at her granddaughter. "I listen to my eyes and nose and fingers, but in the end the mushroom tells me of itself, some secret way. There's no learning the real knack. Your Uncle Emrys says it is much the same with his songs and music. Ah, child, I wish you could hear him! *He* has never sat at a bard's footstool learning meters or been fed by lords as a fee for rhyming flattery." She fluttered her nimble fingers in the air. "It comes to him as a free gift."

"Oh, Mamgu, I wish it went that way with me! Sometimes songs come smooth as butter, but mostly they limp worse than I do. Dad says it's foolishness for a girl to wish to be a poet at all, that only a man can be a bard and compete for prizes in the Eisteddfodau, and if you don't mean to compete, why bother? The meters are so many and so difficult, what with remembering how long each phrase should be and what the orders of rhyming are."

The old lady smiled a secret smile and did a quick half-dance step on her tiny feet with an agility surprising for one of her weight and age.

"Emrys has a silver harp, and yet he never had to spread his music at the feet of know-nothing gentry at an Eisteddfod."

43

"A silver harp? Truly, Mamgu?"

"Aye, truly. How many mushrooms have we in the basket, love? Good, good, that's enough of the sweet caps for now. Come, tell me, my little lame bird, whatever put it in your fair head to be a poetess at all? Not your mam, I warrant. And your dad hasn't a rhyme in his head. Only the gentry have time for such amusement."

"But he does love the hymn singing, Mamgu. And before Anna and Betty were born, on Sundays he carried me across on Caven Gronaunt ferry to the slopes above Pen-

rhyd, where the folk gathered to hear the harpists and
crowthers sing of the old wars against the English and chant
the words of Taliesin and Merlin."

Mamgu paused to wipe her face with the hem of her red
petticoat.

"Ah, Father Merlin." She nodded, obscurely pleased.

Eilian felt a sudden confusion. Looking shyly at her
grandmother, she realized what a strange old woman she
was. The once red-gold hair was wispy and white and cut
short; and her eyes were filmy; and she was fat. But there

was, beneath all that, something else again, as if she were really young and the old-lady shape were only a mummer's costume. Anna and Betty whispered the old stories about the Red Fairies and were frightened of her. They said she mumbled strange words in her sleep.

"Give me your hand here, Eilian. The path is uneven, and if I fell, I should roll all the way to the farmyard gate like a ragged football. Hai, I wish it were not too early in the year for a nice young puffball. They've a lovely taste. Still there should be something interesting to be found. Shall we try our luck over under the witchens? Be looking for something different from what you have in the basket."

"Yes, Mamgu. I once saw a great white fungus over there. Are they for eating, too?"

"Some, some. But some are deadly. And they come later in the summer, not now. Tell me, how shall you like this being a lady and living at Plaseirian? You shall have to take to bathing, and wearing ribbons and gloves, and drinking sweet wine, eh? Hmm. And watch the ladies and gentlemen dancing on the Sunday afternoon grass."

Eilian looked down at her bare feet. The bruise had faded away to a greenish yellow, and the ache was gone, but the lame foot seemed to drag more awkwardly than before. I've been on it too much while it was sore, she thought. Anna and Betty were always begging her help, and she had taken over the milking, churning, and separating. In the evenings, when she tried to use her good foot instead on the treadle of the spinning wheel, it was even more awkward and the thread more uneven.

"What do ladies do if they've maids to tend the animals and spin the flax and wool, Mamgu? They can't be dancing

46

and doing fine needlework all the time. Can they still go walking over the hills and climb trees?"

"I've never seen one do so." Mamgu watched her curiously. "Perhaps they might, with a party of other ladies, and a maid to carry a basket of refreshments."

The way she said "refreshments," tipping her nose in the air and speaking with a delicate affectation, was too much to resist. Eilian laughed and minced ahead, half hopping.

"Will you have a sweetmeat, Mistress Angharad? Such a rich bit of ribbon, Mistress Elizabeth! Where, pray, did you obtain it? At Conwy market or at Wrexham fair? And it came all the way from France? I shall ask Daddy for one directly. What, Mistress Eilian? Climb a tree? How quaint! We shall all help, shan't we? Faith, Mistress Angharad, we'd best send for the cowman to stand under in case she falls, hadn't we?"

Suddenly she stopped in the path and began to weep. Mamgu padded up to fold her in a soft and aromatic embrace.

"Hush, hush. It needn't be as silly as that."

One small hand forced Eilian's chin up, and the other used her apron to dry away the tears. "Poor owlet. It seems there's come an end to freedom for you. It will all be pleasing and obeying and amusing other folk. But there, then! I was forgetting your poems, and so were you. You can sing while the others dance, and recite your bits of verse after supper. All of Caernarvonshire will be wanting to come and listen."

She peered at Eilian with her milky eyes and nodded complacently to herself when the child broke free and, turning her back, began to cry again.

"I don't . . . *want* everyone to listen. It would be . . . it would be as if they were pulling up my breastbone and peering at my heart beneath. They wouldn't *care*. Not really. Some of my songs no one's heard. Not even Mam and Dad. Only me. Only me."

Mamgu clucked sympathetically.

"Ah, yes. Emrys says the same. Our songs are our fruit, and by our fruit we shall be known. But if we do not wish to be known . . . ? For after knowing comes hurting."

"Oh, Mamgu, I love you. I wish I could be with you always. No one else understands. Nor ever did. No one."

"Come, come, come." The old woman stroked her granddaughter's red-gold hair, all the while smiling with a secret satisfaction. She touched Eilian's cheek with the back of her hand, very lightly. "Let's forget the other mushrooms, shall we? Right now the two of us are going to have a proper treat, before the others are home from Conwy market."

In the cool darkness of the sitting room-kitchen, Mamgu cleaned the little mushrooms with a damp cloth. Taking hot water from the kettle that stood at the back of the fire, she set them to boil in a small pot. After several minutes she drained them and put them aside, talking all the while of Emrys, and the forests of the county of Merioneth, and her little home—she called it her "burrow." While she rambled on, weaving the mood of the Great Dark Wood around the shadowy room, in another pot she stirred a scant handful of wheat flour into a generous cupful of sweet cream. When this sauce had thickened, she added the mushrooms and simmered them a few minutes more, adding a pinch of salt. Turned out into warm bowls, the dish filled the room with

48

a delicate and rich fragrance even Mam could not have resisted. Eilian ate hers with the silver spoon and was glad that Mam and the girls weren't at home.

"So much the more for me!" She laughed.

Waking from her half-dreaming remembering of the day, Eilian found that she had thrashed the straw away and was curled up on the hard earth floor of the dairy. Her bad foot, tucked under the other knee, had gone to sleep and felt thick and heavy as an oaken log. When she moved it with her hands, easing it straight, the prickles made her gasp. After they died away, she felt the blood beating heavily across the arch of her foot, an echo to her heart.

Her eyes grew sharper as she strained to see by the moonlight that fell in at the one small window. Dame Alis and her heifer-child dozed in the two stalls across the dairy gutter, standing with eyes closed and muzzles resting on the mangers. Neither would lie down to be a pillow. Alis seemed to have forgotten the old ways now that she had a place of her own. But the mangers gave Eilian an idea, and she busied herself filling the empty one along the front of her own stall with straw. Climbing in was more difficult, and she managed it only at the cost of a scraped shin; but once settled, she could see the stars through the little window above her head. A sound that was half a hum and half a sigh stirred in her. How far away was the sphere where the stars were fastened, she wondered? Too far to fly even if you had as many wings as a seraph, she supposed.

"Who are you, stars light, so bright,
So near, pinned on the far night?

With six seraph wings could I take flight—there?
I wish I may, I might . . ."

It didn't come quite right, but it was fairly close to the
englyn unodl crwca, the crooked one-rhymed *englyn*
where the two lines of the "wings" come first and those of
the "shaft" second. She had never made one before, and
now she repeated it to herself, trying to get it right, hum-
ming aloud on the rhymes.

"Shusha, shusha, does the little owlet whimper in her
sleep?"

It was Mamgu, moving into the stall. Eilian was so startled that she did not think to explain that she'd only been
muttering bits of a song. Her grandmother leaned over the
manger's edge to smooth the hair from her forehead, all the
while keeping up a low, rhythmic crooning. The words
blurred together so that Eilian could make out little more
than the refrain, *hai lwlian hai lwli.* The soft hands moved
up and down her right leg and over her foot, the soft voice
wove sounds, and the milky eyes held her own fast. Eilian
began to be frightened. Mamgu's eyes in the moonlight
were blank and shining, silver, like the fairy dogs' in the old
tales.

The old woman sensed her alarm and broke the spell
with a gentle tap on Eilian's foot. Eilian drew herself to a
sitting position and stared at it. The foot felt warm and
light, and the heavy pulse had dwindled away. As she
peered, afraid to ask Mamgu if it was something she had
done, her alarm became excitement. Her toes had twitched.

"Did you see? They moved," she whispered. "But—
they're no good at all. I *can't* wriggle them. They've no
feeling."

"Try again," said Mamgu. Her voice was low and compelling.

The toes twitched again, slightly.

"Mamgu!"

"There are healing arts your mam and all the doctors in Wales know nothing of," said Mamgu darkly. "And you must not speak of this to her, or to your dad, mind? Or they will not let you come with me."

"With you? *With* you?"

"Yes. To my warm, snug burrow, where you shall eat as you please and play on your Uncle Emrys' harp, and make songs from your secret heart. Emrys and I, we shall make a pet of you."

"I don't understand." Eilian was not sure she was not dreaming. "Dad said I must not stray from the farm, that I shouldn't go even so far as the village, for fear the Rastalls might come to hear of it."

"Aye. But your dad is off to Ludlow tomorrow and won't be here to keep a watch on you. He mistrusts the sharpness of your mam's eye in such things, I think, for when I—oh, very timid I was—when I wondered if a journey to somewhere you'd never been, to be with folk who'd love you dearly, might not be wisest, he was already half persuaded."

Mamgu snorted, covering a laugh with her hand. "Your mam was delighted—half to have you safe, and the other half to be rid of the both of us."

Eilian hesitated. "Mamgu? Why is Mam afraid of us? Sometimes I've almost thought she hated me. But that's not true. She loves me. But she's afraid. She doesn't like to touch me; and she never looks directly at you, only off to one side. Strangers are like that to me, but because I'm lame,

I think. Mam . . . well, I don't know. She can't *really* think I'm change-child, can she?"

"No, no," Mamgu crooned. "She knows you belong to her. You look too much like her brother, your Uncle Emrys, for her to deny her own dear blood. Still . . . faith, that could be it! She was the only darkling among us all, and when she was most miserable, I remember her screaming that she didn't belong to us, that we had stolen her away. From some wealthy and well-born family, I suppose she hoped. She was such a nervous slip of a thing, with dark eyes and a shock of dark hair from the day she was born. But then here you came, fair as could be, the old blood showing up, to prove her sweet daydream a lie."

"Poor Mam." Even as she said it, Eilian felt an uneasy doubt. Resentment might be explained in such a way, but fear? It still made no sense. Unless . . . why should Mam think her folk would steal someone else's child unless . . . unless they were gypsies or fairies? Eilian felt a thrill along her back. The Red Fairies of Merioneth. Old bits of the tales that Dad called rubbish came crowding back. It *was* true. But no, that made no sense either. Why then should she, Eilian, be lame and known for a change-child? If indeed she came of the Fairy Folk, *she* would have been changed for a child who was not lame.

The answer—if answer it was—came as a spiteful whisper at the back of her mind. Since Mam would not admit to being one of the fairies, she would not—as was the custom with the Fair Folk—steal a healthy child and leave her own little weakling in its place.

"No, I'm no change-child," thought Eilian bitterly. "But Mam might be happier if I were."

52

She did not see the look of the-cat-who's-been-at-the-cream on Mamgu's face as she padded to the dairy door and out, on her way back to a cup of mulled ale and bed.

Eilian sat next to Dad in Attorney Llewellyn's coach, a large, shabby, and badly sprung vehicle that rocked with every rut and pebble on the river road. The lawyer, a small, sharp-faced man who smiled more often than his face made you expect, thrust his head out at the window to call to his manservant, riding behind on Dad's pony.

"Dyo? How far do you make it to Llanrwst?"

"Another two miles or thereabouts, Y'r Honor. It's Trefriw we've just passed through."

"Aye, girl," said Dad. "Another good mile and we must put you down to ride with your Mamgu."

"And we shall be sorry to lose your company," the attorney said, with a little ducking bow. "But my poor old coach must keep to the high road. Even if we could spare the time to go by the Falls of the Conwy and east again through Yspytty Ievan after seeing you on your way south, neither it nor my horses could manage that rough and narrow road."

"Yes, sir," Eilian said. "It was kind of you to take me up this far. I never rode in a coach before. It's a bit like being carried in a basket, isn't it?"

"Indeed, and the basket carrier drunk at that," said the lawyer with a laugh. "Your father and I will be sorely jounced before we come to the inn at Pontyla Voelas. Perhaps we should have an early luncheon in Llanrwst instead, eh, Ifan ap Robert?"

"I wouldn't say no to a pint of ale, Mr. Llewellyn. But

the wife's given me a mutton pie here for my noon meal and supper."

"Dad?" Eilian spoke in a whisper. "Tell me again the great towns you will be seeing on your road to Ludlow. What comes after Llangollen?"

"England comes soon after Llangollen: Oswestry and Shrewsbury, I think."

54

"Oswestry." She rolled the word on her tongue. "It's a fairy-tale sort of name."

"And then Church Stretton and Ludlow itself," finished Mr. Llewellyn. "We shall make our depositions and then present our bill of complaint to two or three members of the Council for signature, after which we trot back to wait upon the Clerk of the Signet, to have his deputy pass and seal it. And then your father shall ride home again. I must stay to attend other cases, so I shall be able to find whether Rastall answers the Council's letter missive—that is a summons of sorts, Mistress Eilian. The Council has ways of forcing his attendance more swiftly and effectively than does the common law. He will not dare to ignore the Council as he does the Quarter Sessions in Conwy."

"And if he does appear, Dad? Will you have to ride back to Ludlow again?"

"I fear so. But whether or no, Emrys shall bring you home to Llwyn Cerddin in a fortnight. We'll worry about another journey another time."

The little attorney rubbed his papery hands together. "Yes. Then there will be replications and rejoinders, rebutters and surrejoinders, written interrogatories and depositions, and examinations . . ." He smiled in anticipation of a brisk legal battle.

"Aye," said Dad sourly. "And I am out of pocket tuppence or a shilling in fees every time the Clerk puts his pen to paper."

"The Clerk's deputy's under-clerk, more likely, though most of the fees find their way to the Clerk's—Sir Fulke Greville's—pocket. And there's a shilling or so every time the Examiner questions a witness, as well," Mr. Llewellyn said. "But not to worry. The Council is sure to decide in your favor, in which case they will award you costs."

"Hai! Will that mean Sir Edmund must pay your fees, too?"

"Very likely. Very likely."

The two men roared with laughter. Eilian was fascinated to see her dad so at ease with this droll, precise little man. Mam had been quite the opposite, all formality and fussing, when the coach drew up in the farmyard. In a strained and artificial tone, she had asked after Mrs. Llewellyn and the health of assorted grandchildren, whom she took pains to ask after by name.

Dyo's head appeared at the window again, jogging up and down with the pony's gait.

"Here's Gwydir Castle, sirs, where the little mistress gets down."

Sir John Wynne's castle stood in wide gardens to their left beyond the crossroads. On the right, the wooded hillside and the road for Capel Kerig climbed steeply. Mamgu's little wicker pony cart was drawn up in the shade of a yew tree at the edge of the castle grounds, past the turning the coach was to take for the river crossing and Llanrwst. Mamgu sat holding the reins stiffly, clearly a little put out at not having been able to ride in the coach.

"Come, child, don't dawdle so," she called, as Eilian, having thanked Mr. Llewellyn and been lifted down from the tall step by Dyo, was bidding her father a good-by.

"Take care of yourself now, my girl," said Dad, giving her a hug and a kiss. "We'll see you at home in a fortnight."

"Come along then and put your bundle here beneath the seat," directed Mamgu. "We're off in a hurry, Ifan ap Robert," she said, "for I mean to come to Betws-y-Coed before the rain comes."

56

Dad laughed. "Why, there's not a cloud in the sky, Mamgu."

"Never you mind. There will be."

She flicked her whip at the little pony, and the cart rolled briskly away up the river road. Eilian twisted around on the seat to wave until the coach turned and lumbered out of sight beyond the castle grounds.

"Mamgu?"

"Yes, child?"

Eilian hesitated. "I thought I saw someone coming along after us. On a pony."

Mamgu shrugged. "It's the Queen's highway, and free to all."

"But he didn't turn off to Llanrwst. He's just disappeared."

"Likely whoever it was took the hill road to Capel Kerig. One thing I know it's not. It's not one of the Rastalls' men, so you may rest easy."

She spoke so surely, so complacently, that Eilian turned and settled down to watch the countryside. The valley floor was level and richly green, with the Conwy meandering along it. The thickly wooded hills on the right were steep, and from time to time a rocky ridge or bare summit rose above their dark green. Across the river and beyond the chimneys of Llanrwst, gentler hills rolled away, green with wheat and rye. After a mile or two, Eilian looked back but saw no one.

"I don't care," she thought. "Mamgu may have the second sight and be one of the Fair Folk to boot, but I'm sure someone's still behind."

FOUR

The sense of being watched returned from time to time on the long way into the mountain forests of Merion. But that was not the only strange thing about the journey, which took a good three days longer than Mamgu had told Dad it would, for almost all but the last few miles were traveled on foot. How, Eilian wondered, could she learn even the fingering of the notes on Uncle Emrys' harp if in a handful of days she must turn around to go home? Of course, the going would be faster with her uncle. A good, strong, long-legged man could carry her on his back in the steep places and across the long stretches of boggy moor, which left Eilian's arms and legs sorely midge-bitten and Mamgu's temper as badly frayed as her damp and dragging skirts. There might even be a pony for the going home.

Eilian still did not understand about the pony Mamgu was so angered over. Coming near Capel Betws-y-Coed on that first day, Mamgu had drawn up outside a prosperous-looking cottage and put Eilian down, tossing their bundles after her and directing her to unlatch and open the gate. As she did so, the pony nickered as if he knew the place. It had begun to rain a little, and Eilian, mystified, moved the two bundles beneath a roadside tree. In half a moment Mamgu had driven through the gate, abandoned the pony cart in the courtyard, and was back, snatching up her bundle. She pushed Eilian ahead of her, keeping in the shelter of a hedgerow of hawthorns. Dimly—she could not be sure—Eilian seemed to hear an outcry from behind them, but the rain, coming like a cold and heavy blanket over the hills, drowned what sound there might have been.

They sat out the long rain in a dry, snug, leaf-carpeted chamber deep inside the matted hawthorn hedge. Eilian amused herself by breaking off the dry thorns around the entrance so that they could leave more easily than they had come in. After the storm dwindled to a shower, Mamgu went out "to find us a bit of sustenance." She returned with half an egg pie, a small veal pie, a slab of boulted bread, and a large half-full tankard of beer under her shawl. What they could not eat they tied up in their bundles. Eilian did not notice what became of the tankard when they left. While the last of the rain still spattered, they crossed Pont-y-Pair, the bridge over the Llugwy, and hurried into the little village, which sheltered between the Conwy and the steep hills. But Mamgu seemed to have little liking for streets and houses. Very shortly they took a turning up a lane that climbed out of the town into the damp woods of the hillside. From time to time Eilian had a glimpse of the rooftops strung out along the street as it followed the river below.

"I've a pony waiting for us above the Fairy Glen," said Mamgu when finally they sat down on a fallen tree to catch their breath. "Phew! I should have thought to ask for two. But we shall take turn about, child."

Their road soon dwindled into a footpath that took them down the sharp descent of the Giant's Head. There they had to backtrack a bit to the bridge that crossed the Lledr just above the point where it joined the Conwy. Then, about a quarter mile above the watersmeet, they climbed beside the falling stream through a pretty wooded glen that Mamgu said the townsfolk called the Fairy Glen.

"Which shows how much they know about the Fair Folk," Mamgu said with mingled contempt and spite.

"Mamgu? Will I . . . do you see aught of the Fair Folk in Merion?"

"Only my own Red Fairies," said she slyly. "As for others, some say they've seen 'em, some not."

It was an answer and no answer.

The ravine grew deeper, and in less than a mile white water marked the cascade of waterfalls where the walls of the gorge of the Conwy and the Machno rose steeply, and the road was forced away to the right. The late afternoon shadows quickened Mamgu's steps. Below Machno Mill she came to the footpath she'd been looking for, and with many halts and starts they made it to the hilltop, where Eilian saw a makeshift pen woven of stakes and branches, deep among the trees.

But there was no pony in it.

They stopped there in the pen for the night, eating bits off the bread and pies—with nothing to wash them down— for supper. All the while Mamgu muttered imprecations, waking even in the middle of the night to denounce some unnamed *ynfytyn*, some idiot.

Come morning, they went on, but more slowly. The names of streams and hills meant less and less to Eilian. South from Llyn Conwy, the source of the river, the climbing hills became a drudgery of moors and rocks. Twice it rained heavily when no shelter was at hand, and when the sun returned, it made their garments stink of warm wet wool and then grow stiff. There were wild and rugged mountains in the distance, gashed by deep, gorgelike valleys. The going was almost as difficult through the heavy bracken fern and heather of the moors as in the stretches of rushes and moss and deer grass of the wet upland bogs.

Mamgu kept on somehow, with Eilian trailing behind. The old woman's strength amazed her. It made her feel safe, but it was unnatural. I'm going to be one of the fairies, she thought in the odd detachment of her weariness. She was so turned around—though she knew that they had been working their way south—that she was sure she could never find the way home alone. It was on the afternoon of the third day that, fallen behind to bind up her foot, she caught a glimpse of the follower, a tiny speck of man and pony in the distance. Mamgu stopped at her hail, but when Eilian turned to point, he was gone.

Uncle Emrys came to meet them the next evening, riding a shaggy pony, leading another, and overflowing with apologies.

"I know it all, Mam. I've said it all to myself," he protested, holding his arm before his face as if to ward off Mamgu's angry scolding. "I *had* a pony ready to bring for you to Machno Mill—a good strong little fellow—but it's gone. It was closed with two of Elfodd's in the withy pen near the dingle, but when I went at dawn five days past to fetch it, all three were gone. The fence was torn to pieces. I think it was not the Overseer," he said pointedly. "I think it may have been the Children that freed them."

"Hush you," said Mamgu wearily, her indignation spent. "Well, you're better late than *too* late, I suppose. Where are these two from? Llanfachrueth way? Hmph. Come then, get you down and give us a hand. Did you think to bring any victuals?"

Emrys, dismounting, laughed and touched the bulging wallet that hung at his side. "I knew it was you I was coming for, Mam. There's the end of a mutton roast, a bottle of sour milk, and a loaf of white bread."

"*White* bread?" Mamgu gave him a push on the chest. "And where did you find white bread, Emrys bach?"

Eilian liked her uncle's laugh. It was warm and soft.

"I've not stolen it, Mam, I promise you," he teased. "I traded a kiss for it with the kitchen slavey at Perllan House."

"That's worse," Mamgu grumbled. "Come, you've not said boo to your niece. Eilian Roberts, here is your silly uncle, Emrys ap Gruffydd."

"Good day, Uncle." Eilian made an uncertain curtsy. How did one greet a strange, small, brown-skinned, red-haired uncle as oddly clad as this one, who rode a pony with ribbons knotted in its mane? Emrys wore a longish blue shirt belted with a tatty silk cord and, over it, a patchwork mantle of green and blue and brown. More, he was barelegged, without breeches or hose, in the fashion of the days before Queen Mary's time.

"And the best of days to you, good niece," he said, falling to one knee and taking her hand to kiss it with a gentle-

62

manly air at once sweet and comical. Hand on his heart, he recited:

> "I wallt fal tafod o aur,
> i dal fal llygaid y dydd.

> "Her tresses a tongue of gold,
> Her brow like the daisies."

"That's quite enough," said Mamgu, her humor restored. "Leave off your laughing and help me up onto this poor creature who must carry me. And cut me some bits of supper to go on."

At the end of dusk they came to the crown of a hill, which rolled down from their ponies' feet long and gently to a far row of low hummocky hillocks. Beyond these a great dark forest stretched across a wide and rolling plain from the eastern mountains to the borders of the foothills below the western ridges.

"The Great Dark Wood," Mamgu said. Her voice held as much unease as pleasure. "I could wish we had come before sunset."

"Our way bends westward, across the foothills," Emrys explained to Eilian, sitting behind him on the larger pony. "Our home is at the southern rim of the Great Wood."

"Is there no path through the forest? It must be twice as far to go the long way around."

"No. That is, there *may* be a path." He was evasive, but then brightened, saying, "But we've no lantern, and even the moon when she comes up could not light us under that heavy roof of leaves."

Riding down out of the foothills in the moonlight, they

63

were met by a swarm of lights bobbing up from under the eaves of the wood like a flight of fireflies.

"No, dear Queen," someone called, "it's us, not the Overseer!"

The voice floated up the hill with echoes of laughter, and in a moment they were surrounded by ten or a dozen men and women, some smaller even than Mamgu and Emrys. Some were young and some older, but none so old as Eilian's grandmother. There were laughs and greetings and kisses, and in the light of the lanterns their hair shone gold and their eyes gleamed silver. Eilian tightened her arms around her uncle's waist until he could feel her heart pounding from fear and excitement. "Maybe I'll never go home," she thought. "Maybe, maybe this is the true home-coming." Mam and Dad seemed dim shadows in a heavier world.

The company moved into the wood, some singing as they walked. A few of the snatches of song were what Mam called "coarse," and at a sharp word from Mamgu the singers slid good-humoredly into a bit of nonsense that left Eilian amazed and mystified:

> "A lych gate, fishnets, wicker,
> birds and thickets,
> A hillock, a mill, a bullock,
> And look—buckets of toads and nuts!"

A few hundred yards into the wood, the ground fell away into a deep dingle the shape of a giant bowl broken on the one side where water from a small spring flowed out into the darkness. A great fire burned in the clearing below. Once the ponies were tethered to a tree, the company followed Mamgu into the hollow. The path curved down from the rim and, along its upper portion, was partly screened by young birches. Here and there on the opposite side Eilian could see black holes, which looked to be small caves. Those at the bottom of the slope were larger, with log doorposts and lintels and rough gutters to keep the rain from running in. Even stranger were the hummocks dotting the bottom of the hollow. They turned out to be sod roofs, and under each was a little low door into a windowless room dug deep enough below the level of the ground for a small man to stand upright inside. A woman with a baby sat in front of one of the doorways, and a woman of middle age sat tending the fire and turning the heavy iron spit.

The others crowded close around the fire, and Eilian could only nod as Mamgu introduced her to each in turn. Each face was, in a clear or in a distant way, an image of her own as she had seen it reflected in the spring at Llwyn Cerddin. The circle of firelight was echoed in the circle of red-gold locks around her—in the long braids or loosely twisted locks of the women and girls, and the elf locks and matted curls of the men. Some of the young men and women wore silver rings in their hair, and one pretty young woman with hair that hung below her waist had twined it around with ribbons and gold thread. Their clothing made the dingle a shimmering, iridescent pool of scarlet, of plum and wine colors, of blues and greens. Sleeves of one color, bodices another, tunics mended with bits of ribbon, and cloaks of patchwork silks and woolen stuffs—it made the scene more like a dream than dreams were. The folk were beautiful, far more beautiful than all the Queen's officers and the ladies and gentlemen riding in their finery beneath Caernarvon's towers.

". . . Elis and Ysfael, Gwladus, Gwennol, and here is Pilipala in all her ribbons. But you will never remember so many names. You may call them all cousin," said Mamgu. "They are that, for the most part—cousins second, third, and fourth, and once and twice removed!"

Amid the laughter, Uncle Emrys brought a silver cup and a pitcher from one of the huts. Pilipala held the cup while he poured and then brought it to Eilian. She made a deep curtsy as she offered it, sweeping her ribbons to the ground and smiling.

"A cup of sweet mulled wine to wash away the journey, Cousin Eilian, and to welcome you home to the Red Fairies."

Late as it was, after the greetings came a feast—succulent geese and chickens that turned on the spit next to the large side of mutton; a caudle of young parsnips and onions; slices of porridge cut cold from the bowl, fried in butter, and sugared; mulled wine, and a small barrel of ale said to be the gift of the squire of Perllan.

"He is a generous squire, then?" Eilian asked shyly.

The laughter and singing faltered, and Uncle Emrys' humorous face was emptied of its warmth. While he stared into his cup, Eilian half fancied an emptiness, a blankness where resentment and confusion were being forced down and away, buried, but only with a great effort. He drained the cup quickly and signed to Pilipala for more.

It was Mamgu who answered Eilian's question. "Generous? Yes, for he is rich and to spare. And he will be more generous still when he returns from his journeying."

"Not if he knew how much he had spared already," someone whispered behind her, with a half-muffled snort.

"Shut you up, Ysfael!" Mamgu snapped. "You do not amuse us."

Ysfael, who had thought himself unheard, was covered with confusion. Gwennol, the girl Eilian took to be his wife, gave a nudge and a whisper, and he darted off to one of the burrows, returning with a violin, a *crwth*. Gwennol moved to stand in front of Mamgu's seat, laughter in her eyes, silently questioning.

At the old woman's nod, harp, cornet, recorders, a battered flute, and a second *crwth* appeared. The company fell silent, waiting. Mamgu rose, spoke a greeting or command —Eilian could not tell which—in a strange gibberish string of words, and raised her hand. At the gesture, the fire flamed high, licking at the night sky with bright tongues of blue and rose and green. Music climbed with it, and a dance that seemed itself to be a fire.

It was a strong and swelling music, *crwth* and harp and wind instruments braided in song with rich, sweet voices. It pulled Eilian to her feet, straining upward as if she would fly on the strength of her heart's desiring, her hands clasped together fiercely, as if by pushing against herself she could rise in the air with the lovely wildness of the music or whirl into the dance that wove a shimmering band of light around the strange cup of a valley. Among the dancers some appeared to fly. Eilian's head swam so from weariness, from the rich food and drink, and from the spell of color and sound that afterward she was not sure she had not dreamed it. Yet it had seemed that Gwennol, darting like the swallows she was named for, had flown high across the fire from where Elis stood, to light in Ysfael's arms. "And she has not wings," thought Eilian, dazzled. She swayed. "Why could I not dance, then?"

Emrys, who sat in solitary gloom against one of the hovels, his silver harp silent beside him and a cup half empty in his hand, stretched out the other as if to stop her, but she was beyond his reach. One lovely, dipping whirl of a step,

and then the child's weak foot gave way and she fell into the ashes at the fire's cold edge.

In a flash he ran to scoop her up and sat with her in his arms, going on with the song in his deep, smooth voice. The others, scarcely missing a beat, obeyed his gestured sign to continue.

"Come, wipe the wonder from your eyes, little bird," he whispered. "Not all things are as they seem. Tinsel is flimsy beside true metal; and the tree which grows wildest often bears the crabbed fruit."

"What do you say? What is it you are whispering there?" Mamgu plucked at his sleeve.

"Why, nothing, Mam." He turned his blue-gray eyes up to meet her milky stare and answered calmly. "The child has wearied herself to sleep, and I was only after saying how glad I was to have such a pretty one come among the Red Fairies."

"Mm, well." Mamgu settled back on her low seat, full and at ease, looking more like a plump, ruffled black mushroom than ever, but—Emrys thought—most of all like a sleepy spider at the center of a glistening, iridescent web.

FIVE

It was the sixth morning. Or was it the seventh? The strange rhythm of life in the Dark Wood still eluded Eilian. One day was like another, and one familiar face was mirrored in the next. Yet while she was not sure whether the sameness of days—for all their warmth and pleasure—was one of emptiness or fullness, gradually patterns did appear. In the mornings she sat with Pilipala, or sometimes with one of the others, stitching or plucking fowl and learning their songs. Pilipala was nearest her own age—"Sixteen or seventeen by Mamgu's guess," Pilipala had said. Unlike the others, she was always to be found somewhere in the dingle: mending a tunic with scraps of ribbon, cleaning a chicken, or basting mutton on the spit. For all her ribbons and striking looks, she was quiet, shy almost.

Mamgu herself rose in midmorning and would spend an hour, perhaps more, stroking and kneading the muscles of Eilian's lower leg and foot until it seemed to glow. Gradually, Eilian came to feel Mamgu's pinches along the underside of the toes so clearly that she cried out. At times Mamgu used her sleeve for rubbing or the back of a knife, sometimes a rag soaked in an infusion of herbs. Afterward, she always replaced the red string she had tied around the thin ankle, and one of the young men carried Eilian to the spring, where her foot was thrust into the chilly water. She was not allowed to walk there herself, though the distance was short.

"Keep off the foot," Mamgu insisted. "We must go carefully, gently, and not ask too much of it too soon."

Because of the pleasure of the rubbing and the constant laughter and movement of life in the dingle, with so many willing hands to fetch for her and arms to carry her, she obeyed. Once in a while her gaze wandered up the slopes to the birches and beeches on the high rim, and once Elis carried her downstream from the spring through the rushes and ferns to see the lilies that bloomed along the banks of the larger stream fed by their own. But she had not really seen the forest itself, and gradually she came to understand that the others feared it and never went farther in than their own valley. Why this was, she could not find out. It was not for fear of wild boars or other beasts. There seemed, in fact, to be no beasts at all but the squirrels on which they dined one day when there was no mutton or fowl. Eilian had asked several of the cousins why they did not explore further, but their answers were evasive. One said it was because of the "Overseers," and another that "the Children are said to have forbidden it." But she could learn nothing of who these folk were, the Overseers and the Children. Mamgu turned her questions away and dismissed her wish to walk in the woods by saying that it was only a wood like other woods.

"You must not be restless. Mamgu knows best," she said.

Once, Eilian found herself wondering whether Mamgu *did* know best, and immediately felt ashamed. Still, it did seem almost that in keeping Eilian always under her eye, Mamgu was more concerned for her own convenience than for her granddaughter's well-being. Cosseted and kept inactive, Eilian found it very hard *not* to be restless.

Yesterday, and once before that, new faces—still familiar —had appeared and others had gone. Gwennol and Ysfael and several others had departed with their horns and harps and a *crwth*, and strangers had come, clad in rags of gray and brown. Some wore dirty bandages, and others carried rude crutches; but they sang and capered down the path to bow and scrape in fun at Mamgu's feet, heaping their bulging bags and wallets by her seat. When at mealtime the company gathered again, even these were as splendid as the others in their bright embroidered gear, with red-gold hair new-washed and shining. And both times there had been gifts all around. Eilian had been given a silver comb and a gold ring, and Mamgu wore a new black felt hat and shoes with silver buckles.

Eilian shifted uncomfortably on her bed, a sweet-smelling heap of pine boughs covered with skins and a much-patched woolen rug. Was it that they were come to beggary then, that some went disguised in rags and bandages? If that was so, it was odd that they did not speak of it, for begging was respectable enough. At Conwy on a market day, the gentry were greeted by beggars at every gate of the old town, and in Anglesey it was a way of life for many of the poor. Newly wed beggar couples went begging for a season and then could set up housekeeping after a fashion, even if not very comfortably. The English law had tried to put a stop to it all, but as Dad had said, the Welsh gentry weren't about to shut up their purses and their larders because the English told them to. Still, Eilian had not thought that fairies would live such a ramshackle life or that ladies gave away silver combs and gold rings.

A shadow at the doorway stopped the drift of her thoughts. Emrys had popped his head in to see if she was stirring yet and made as if to slip away again unnoticed. But Eilian, putting a finger to her lips, sat upright and swung her legs to the floor. Mamgu snored gently and shifted on her bed in the burrow's darkest corner, but did not wake.

Eilian hopped to the door, and Emrys helped her up and out, kneeling so that he could take her on his back.

"I've missed you, Uncle," she said in his ear. "You're never here. Are you angry that I've come? Pilipala says that you are always full of songs and funning, but that you are changed. And I had hoped so that you would teach me something of the harp. It's *not* my coming, is it?" She pulled at a lock of his hair.

"Pilipala ought not say such things to you," he muttered.

The valley was still asleep except for one young man carrying firewood from a store in one of the caves and another cousin laying a fresh fire. Emrys carried Eilian toward the log seat by the spring, where their talking would disturb no one.

"But Pilipala worries for you, Uncle. Does that so displease you?" She leaned over his shoulder and caught sight of the grin that tugged at the corner of his mouth.

"I thought not!" She laughed.

"And how should you know so much about it, owlet?"

73

"It is in the way you watch her when she dances, Uncle. Why don't you marry her?"

He threw his head back and laughed aloud. "I'd like nothing better," he said, and made as if to put her down on the log. "And you must call me 'Emrys,' if you please. 'Uncle' makes me stoop with age."

"Oh, there! You very near cracked my nose!" She giggled and would not be put down, but wound her arms more tightly around his neck. "Please . . . Emrys? Mamgu won't wake for hours. Will you not take me up into the wood? This once? I've seen nothing of it, and I'm to go home soon. None of the others will take me up, but they will not tell if it's you who do. Mamgu wouldn't scold you."

He laughed ruefully, she thought.

"You ought not tease as if you were a baby," he chided, hoisting her up again more securely. "Unh! And you are too heavy to be carried about like one. Indeed, you'll be a woman soon."

"Oh, but then teasing's more fun than ever, from what I've seen among the lads and maids at home," she whispered. "Why doesn't Pilipala know that? Doesn't she know you watch her? Shall I tell?"

Emrys gave a snort that was only half a laugh and a sign with his free hand that she should hold her tongue. As if to make sure she did, he ran up the curving path toward the wood above at a brisk trot. At the top of the hill, screened from eyes below by a clump of young birches, he paused for breath, then went on more slowly. They followed a path that wandered around tangles of undergrowth and wound among the trees in the seemingly aimless manner of a deer track.

74

"*Are* there deer here, Emrys?"

"Once, perhaps, but no more. No, these are paths made Red-Fairy fashion here on the borders of the wood, so that strangers will mistake them for paths the beasts have made."

"What strangers? The Overseers?" She hazarded a guess.

Emrys set her down on the path and, taking her by the shoulders, looked at her curiously, closely.

"Who has been telling you of the Overseers? What have they told you?"

"No one and nothing." She sighed. "About so many things."

"Yes, well." He rubbed a finger under his nose. "Mamgu will have it so. And Eilian? You must take care to say nothing of me to Pilipala, or of her to Mamgu. If we are to be friends, you must promise that."

"But why, Emrys, if you wish to marry her?"

Her uncle shook her sharply. "Because Mamgu would send Pilipala away! Do you promise?"

"Oh, yes!" But she was bewildered. "*Why* would she? Is it like with me? That Mamgu loves you but doesn't care about your heart? For I am kept from the wood, from walking or being off alone with many of the cousins—even from the aloneness with myself where poems grow."

His frown cleared slowly, and he smiled, as if her words had freed him somehow. They began, very slowly, to walk among the beeches away from the path.

"Yes, it is just so with me," Emrys said. "With all of us. We are bound to her as if she were as much a queen as that other red-haired one, Sidanen—Queen Elizabeth—on her throne in London."

"Is she not truly Queen of the Red Fairies, then?"

"Oh, she *is* that, but Eilian . . . do you not know that that—well, that it is only a manner of speaking? We . . . What is it? What do you see?"

Eilian pointed to a gap in the trees south toward the forest's edge.

"Is that one of the Overseers?"

She had hardly spoken the words when Emrys scooped her up and plunged into a low thicket.

"Where?" he hissed, covering their heads with his cloak. "There? Ah, what a turn you gave me! It's only Elfodd, on watch."

The unease that had hovered near her for days was suddenly a sharp suspicion and then a certainty. Eilian wriggled free and, limping a few steps from the thicket, turned suddenly to face him.

"Are the Overseers constables' men, then? And do they come after folk who eat mutton and fat capons and eggs, but keep no sheep nor fowl? And who have bread and porridge in plenty, but work no fields of oats and corn?"

Emrys laughed but sobered fast enough when he saw her distress.

"Aye, and who ride ponies they never saw foaled," he agreed.

"And who are the Children?"

Looking over his shoulder, Emrys seemed to hesitate and then, grim-faced, picked her up and strode away from the sun-dappled slopes through the green light that glowed among the beeches, into the Dark Wood. When they had gone a short distance into its stillness, he set her down to walk along beside him.

76

"Yes, put your weight on it," he said roughly, and pulled her along. He ignored the question about the Children. "If you don't use the strength you have, all the cosseting and rubbing in the northern hills will not keep it from wasting away. You'll come to lean on your Mamgu as we all have, until you can't stand without her." He squeezed her hand. "I was sorry indeed when I saw how little you knew about us. You see, your mam ran away a year before our father was hung for a sheepstealer, and she'll have thought we all escaped the old ways without him to rule us. But for all Mamgu's railing at the old man, when he was gone she knew no other way to live. Your guess is tardy but true. The Overseers answer to the Justice of the Peace. Oh, Merioneth is famous for her thieves," he said bitterly. "We've more Justices of the Peace than any county in Wales, and instead of a constable who enlists a farmer or two when he has need of them, we've the Overseers after us all the time."

He sat down on a stone and ran his fingers through his bright hair. Plaintively, he said, "If we weren't pushed so hard, we could catch our breath. Maybe go north and make an honest living with our music and the begging." He looked up, pleading. "We try sometimes. You've not heard better minstrels or seen better dancers and acrobats, have you now? It was Mamgu's thought long ago that we might be escaping this life that way, but we've not kept to it."

It was all too much to take in at once. Emrys looked so forlorn that Eilian was torn between laughing and crying.

"Then," she said, turning slowly, drawing a ring around her with her right foot, "then we're not fairies?"

He looked at her helplessly.

"Is it such a disappointment? But how can you have

thought we truly were? The Fair Folk are cold and hard, and hurtful, if the old tales are true. You see, after our fathers and mothers found our den here near the woods' edge, they heard old tales of the Dark Forest that had come down from shepherds to their sons, and they—they took advantage of them. The Fair Folk have a name for thievery and music, and so long as the simple folk from here to Dolgellau knew of us as the Red Fairies, they took care not to offend us. Time was when even the constables turned their backs. But the Overseers have more suspicious minds. None have pursued us into the wood yet, but they keep a watch at the south ford of the river, and even along the western foothills. One day they will be bolder. What's to happen to us then, I don't know. Your Mamgu has something hatching, but I mistrust it. There's an ache in my bones that fears she's up to no good. You'll be well away from us, child."

"But you have just said that I am beyond being a child." She drew herself up. "I may be small, but I'm past twelve winters old. Girls wed at thirteen. Some do, you know."

"Aye, and it's a sad thing," he said flatly. "Their fathers make alliance with rich yeomen or great families, not caring if they've shackled a fledgling nightingale to a sparrow hawk. No, child, this life here's a snare for pretty birds. They do not leave it when they can, and when they would, they cannot."

"Then I shall see the wood before I go!"

She hopped aside and ran, her right heel kicking awkwardly out. Disappointment and relief together drove her from her uncle. She had wanted to go home, and yet she did not. She felt a rush of hatred for Mamgu and Emrys and all of the cousins. Why could people not be as they seemed?

78

For their seeming was so beautiful. To be at the center of their easy warmth was like butter and cream after so many sour seasons of spinning and hoeing and watching the sheep on the high pastures. Animals were warm and kind; and Dad of course, but to have thought that so many others were . . .

Eilian slowed as Emrys came beside her. She saw his concern and after a moment's hesitation gave him her hand. Almost she felt that he was the child, that all the cousins were lost children. Emrys seemed to hang back as they walked—reluctant, fearful, and yet helpless to stop her. There was no undergrowth here; no sunlight. Only towering green-boled beeches, tall quickbeams—or witchens, as Mamgu called them—and ash trees, marching in a green light, as if these were the slopes and dales of a wood at the bottom of the sea.

They came to a stream that ran among mossy rocks between banks hung with ferns, and Emrys would go no farther.

"The rocks are too slippery. We could not cross even if we wished."

Eilian turned to protest, but before the words came, she heard a distant horn. The sound was faint but clear. It was repeated twice and then three times more. Emrys grasped her arm.

"It is our alarm! Or a signal to Mamgu."

"Quickly, then. Take me up on your back."

He hesitated. "But if it were the Overseeers, or soldiers. . . . No, you are safer here. I will see what it is and return as quickly as I can. But *do* not leave the stream, or I will never find you."

The flicker of blue and green and brown that was his cloak melted into the shadows of the wood, and the stillness came lapping around Eilian's feet. She found a flat, dry stone atop a heap of mossy ones beside the stream and sat there, listening until she could almost hear her own blood beating. The horn did not sound again.

She looked around her. All was cool and clear and clean, as if it were a world new-made or freshly washed. No weeds, no dust, no confusion. In its still perfection it began to be a little frightening. The deeper the wood, the darker this green light. No, not darker. Somehow it was not that. The deeper the wood, the *deeper* the light, as if somewhere farther in there was the center of all greenness.

> "At the dark wild's thick-limbed center
> Grows a tree from which all others spring,"

she sang, made uneasy by the silence.

> "Beyond the withy-woven edge
> The thickets fail, the world's shut out,
> So here I sit and watch the watery light,
> Trees gowned in green, trunks of ash and silver,
> In the cool sweet gloom."

"But the dark lies before the wood," came an answer, singing through the forest like a peal of silver.

A slim figure—and a pony—stood on the opposite bank. It was a dark and slender boy, gray-eyed, and wrapped in a cloak of heather colors. After her first alarm, Eilian stared. The pony had the look of one of the mountain ponies from the Caernarvonshire hills.

"Why, it was you following us a week past! Do I know you, then? Or you me? Who are you?"

"Have you forgotten so soon, then? My pony has a better memory, for you are the only maid he ever carried. We heard your song and came to you. It had a sweet tone and a pleasant thought, but little shape," he said with a mischievous grin.

At that, and the sound of his voice, she knew him. It had been dark that last time, and she had not seen him clearly.

"Goronwy! It *is* you. But why are you here? Why have you come?" She stepped into the water to cross to him.

"Like you, I have kinfolk hereabouts," he said with a faint smile. "But have you not lost a handful of days? It was not a week ago that I came this way behind you. You set out from Llwyn Cerddin near three weeks ago."

"But that can't be . . . " she began, reaching out for his hand.

Just as they touched, she heard behind her Emrys' cry of alarm.

"Eilian, child! No, come away!"

Both the boy Goronwy and the pony stiffened slightly, and Eilian turned in surprise.

"But this is . . . Goronwy, a friend of mine, Uncle," she protested, wondering at the pallor of Emrys' face and the tremor of the strong hands that reached down to lift her from the water.

"A friend?" His voice shook. "Since when does friendship with the Children come on such short acquaintance?"

"The *Children?*"

Eilian whirled, but Goronwy and his pony were gone. The wood was as still as if they had never been.

Eilian's thoughts sped as Emrys strode through the wood, bearing her on his back. If he would answer no questions, she could puzzle it out for herself. He had mistaken Goronwy for one of the Children and feared him. In her mind's eye she saw Goronwy again: dark-haired, gray-eyed, with milk-white skin, wearing a cloak that would have been invisible against a mountain hillside. It made no sense. He had carried no weapon, made no threat. Why should Emrys have feared him? Unless the Children were . . . *y Tylwyth Teg yn y Coed* . . . the *Bendith y Mamau!* The Good Little Children of the old tale? The Children of the Great Dark Wood, the Fair Folk? Even if the cousins had never seen them and did not know, that at least must be what they thought and why they feared. Yet to mistake Goronwy for one of the Fair Folk? He was neither cold nor hurtful. But she decided to let it rest.

"What did the horn sound for, Uncle? Had something gone amiss?"

"No." He sounded preoccupied, as if he wrestled with other thoughts. "It was Penry, the steward at Perllan House, come to summon Mamgu. Odd, it was. The women had to rouse her from her bed, but she seemed not to mind. She took a pony and went to meet him at the ford."

"Perllan? That is where you kissed the kitchen maid? Is it far?"

"Yes and no." He laughed, his humor somewhat restored. "That is, yes and yes. As the crow flies, Perllan House must be six miles, but by the road it is nearer ten. Mmm. I cannot think why he should have wished to see Mamgu."

Mamgu had not returned by noon, and still was gone at sunset. The cousins had given her up and were in the middle of their meal when she appeared on the path, helped down by Elis, who had been on guard above.

"Our Queen came with Penry and two pikemen for

guards! Was ever such a sight? And they bowed to her when they parted at the ford," he announced excitedly to the company, much to Mamgu's annoyance.

She was surrounded and pelted with questions, for she wore a new mantle of soft blue woolen stuff lined with dark red silk and carried a bundle wrapped in her old cloak.

"The Squire has come home to Perllan at long last," was all that she would say. "And he remembers old friends. Come, back to your meal. I've supped already, but when I've put my new cloak away, I'll take a nice crusty bit off the mutton. And we must break out the last of the wine, Emrys, for tomorrow is home-going day for our Eilian!"

There were groans for the news and cheers for the wine, and Eilian, who had hung back at first, ran to throw her arms around Mamgu. Yesterday she would not have thought "home-going" to be such a sweet word. "No," she said to herself fiercely: "bittersweet." Mamgu stroked her hair and said she hoped Eilian would not forget her old grandmother when she was rich and lived in a great house. Everyone cheered again, but more self-consciously.

It was only afterward, in the dark, when the fire and the music had died down and she tried to count the days, that Eilian felt a nagging unease. How many *had* it been? Twelve by Mamgu's count; but Goronwy said nearer twenty. She could not sort it out. The tea Mamgu had brewed from herbs to help her sleep had fuddled her wits, and she slid over the edge of sleep still counting.

SIX

At dawn Emrys came to the head of the pass and dismounted to rest his pony before their descent into the valley of the Lliw. From his wallet he took a packet wrapped in a scrap of cloth, unwound it slowly, and ate a handful of the crumbled oatcake it held. Still holding the pony's halter rope, he sat on a tussock of grass to watch the vale below emerge, gray-green, from the night's shadows. The dingle would be stirring soon, he thought. He had listened at Mamgu's door before his leaving, but the sound of Eilian's breathing had been so deep and slow that he could not bring himself to wake her from such a sleep to say farewell. He hoped the child's father would not be too angered with her grandmother for keeping her so long and sending no word, but at least Mamgu would be there to make her own excuses. Emrys was glad of that, if nothing else. He had no wish to face his sister's husband. To explain Mamgu's actions was never easy.

Nor was it now. He felt the sealed letter under his tunic and wondered again why Perllan's squire should be sending a message eastward to the town of Bala by such messengers

85

as Mamgu and now himself. He took it out and weighed it in his hand. It was impressive looking enough to be as important as Mamgu said it was: a heavy, expensive paper it was, folded several times and sealed with a ribbon and a fat blob of sealing wax printed with a strange device: a flame circled by the inscription IC·RASETTE. Why—if it were a matter as urgent as Mamgu said—had the Squire not sent it directly, by one of his own men? Mamgu insisted he must rise at middle-night to be at Bala in time. Emrys frowned. He misliked the idea of riding into Bala at all. The town would be full of Justices of the Peace and justices, perhaps even law officers who could recognize him, for the court of the Great Sessions would be sitting now. The letter was addressed *Myles Tuder, Esquire*. This Tuder might himself be one of the Queen's officers for all Mamgu seemed to know. "Hand it to Squire Tuder in private," was all she would say. He had protested that Elis could take it as well and that another journey to Roe Wen was too much for an old woman. He would gladly take Eilian home as he had promised. Mamgu had not answered, but fixed him with her milky stare as if he were a contentious child she was too fond of to rebuke in front of the others and in the midst of festivity. So, when the child fell off to sleep, he had carried her to her bed and kissed her and then gone to his own.

Emrys came to the end of the oatcakes. He folded the wrapping and stuffed it into his wallet and the letter back into his tunic. "Come, little mare," he said, pulling himself up. "It would be fine to wait here for the sun, but we cannot." He mounted and turned the pony's head toward the downhill track.

Behind, somewhere overhill the way they had come, a

whistle sounded: three notes, thin and sweet, on the edge of hearing.

"There's an odd bird," said he, aloud, as he gave the little mare a brisk thump on the ribs to set her on her way. But she would not move.

The odd whistle came once again, clear, but as if it rang more in the mind than in the ear. While Emrys sat astride her, dumbfounded, his pony turned, ears forward, and began to pick her way back up the path.

"Drato! What's got into you? Come, back you go!"

But no urging or beating would turn her. She came to the crest between the bare hills and stood, trembling, to wait the rider who came up out of the gloom below.

Emrys muttered a blessing under his breath and tried to pull the pony's head around toward their eastward way. Her neck was like iron, and there was nothing to do but stand. In the cloaked figure that approached them, coming like a shadow on the heather hill, Emrys recognized the child of the wood Eilian had called Goronwy. In dismay, and a little fearing, he felt at his side for his knife. The Fair Folk, it was said, could not bear the touch or sight of iron.

"Keep off! Free my pony and we will not hinder your passing," he cried.

The boy—for, Emrys thought, he did seem only a boy—kept on until he came level with the other's spellbound pony.

"Keep your *ceffyl-dwr* from my mount, then," protested Emrys, moving from fear to the edge of anger. "I mislike elvish water-horses."

"He is only half *ceffyl-dwr*," said Goronwy calmly. "He'll do you no harm. And I do not wish to pass, for my

business is with you. If you care for the maid who calls you uncle, I give you warning.

> "The way north
> By the road south

Draws the nightingale forth
Into the cruel hawk's mouth.

"Make of that what you will. You will know what to do
if you are all a man, and your own."

As abruptly as he had spoken, he was gone. Back the way of the Dark Wood, Emrys thought, but in his confusion he was not sure. The strangeness of the encounter held him, amazed. When at last he came to himself, he gave a shake like a dog come out of the water. The pony, waking, turned again toward the valley of the Lliw.

As they went, Emrys, moved to a deep unrest, whispered the riddling verse to himself again and again. Something of the way—Goronwy?—something in his manner made Emrys fear he would be the happier for not unraveling its meaning.

Pilipala awakened from an uneasy sleep only an hour after Emrys' leaving to find the little valley stirring already. Mamgu, who never rose before the sun was halfway to noon, moved—like a black hole in the dingle's darkness—from hovel to burrow, rousing the women. Those with husbands she silently warned against waking their men.

"Hai!" she exclaimed when she saw Pilipala still in her cloak, curled atop her blankets. "Have you been out prowling in the dark of the moon, my pretty one?"

"I . . . I woke at middle-night and heard Emrys bring his pony down." She faltered. "And after I'd gone out to see who it was, I thought it no harm to walk with him downstream a way."

"No, no harm," said Mamgu vaguely. "A way? How far a way?"

"Past the upper crossing. To the eastern trail at the edge of the forest." Pilipala could feel her heart shrink beneath the gaze she felt but could not see.

"A tender parting, I warrant. And did he kiss you?" The words writhed like snakes in the air.

"Oh no, ma'am!" she protested, truly frightened. "Never. He never did!"

"Well, no harm done." The words came slowly and softly. "Come, we must ready Eilian for her home-going. We must be away at dawn, for we are expected at a certain time, you see." Her voice trailed off, and then she added, thoughtfully, "And you had best do all of your things up into a bundle, my dear."

Pilipala's heart grew still and heavy, a leaden weight beneath her breastbone. "Am I to go with you all the way, then?"

"Aye. Aye. It will do you good to see some of the world, my girl."

While Eilian still slept, lamps were lit and the fire kindled. Parties were sent, a lantern with each, to fetch the ponies down from the pen above and to pick flowers and leafy branches along the stream below. Mamgu brought out the cloak-wrapped bundle she had carried home from Perllan House, producing from it an old-fashioned dress of white damask and a pair of satin slippers. She set one of the cousins to work with needle and thread to make the dress smaller in the bodice, and the others were put to braiding ribbons in the ponies' manes. Those who had gone for flowers returned with armloads of lilies and willow branches.

"The flowers are all tightly closed, Mamgu," they said, using the name as a title of respect as was their custom. "We could find only these in the dark."

"They will do well enough," the old woman said. "Make yourselves useful by twining them into wreaths and garlands."

The older women exchanged puzzled glances, but the younger ones set themselves to work at once, thinking it a pretty idea to give the little one such a farewell. Except for Pilipala. Was it only chance that Emrys had been sent away on the day he had thought to be taking his niece home? Pilipala was sure from the polite and distant way Mamgu spoke to her as she worked at a willow garland that she was being sent away for fear Emrys loved her. Mamgu would make certain that she did not come back. And because Emrys had never touched or spoken to Pilipala as he felt, he would slowly be won to thinking Mamgu had done it all for the best. Had *he* been sent away for some such reason? Or was it something to do with Eilian? The child was fond of her Uncle Emrys, and he of her. What was the old woman up to?

Wisely, Pilipala concealed her misgivings and asked no questions. "At least I shall be with Eilian in Emrys' place," she told herself. What good that might do she did not know, but the thought that she might stand for him in this small thing lifted her spirits a little.

Eilian half woke to a dizzying bustle. She felt as if she were back in the dream world of that first night. There were lights flaring in the grayness before dawn, cousins in their parti-colored finery, ponies decked with wreaths and streamers—an unreal scene played in silence, like a masque without music. Everything was blurred at the edges, and the lamps hurt her eyes with their brightness.

"Must I come out, Mamgu? It's night yet. Must I come out?" She swayed slightly, holding to the doorpost.

"Hush, you'll wake the menfolk." Mamgu whispered.

"Yes, my sweet bird. We must be ready to leave with the dawn, and you must be washed and properly clothed."

Eilian shook her head slightly, as if to clear it. "What's the need to go so early? With the ponies, tomorrow eve will bring me home. Where is Emrys? He'll tell you that. I only want to sleep. So sleepy. My head hurts." She pressed her eyes with her fingers, and the ache seemed to lessen. "Go away," she said, and turned back to her bed, curling up as a dog will do in a cold room.

"Poor little one," Mamgu said softly, pleading, almost as if against her will. "I am sorry for your aching head. But . . . but you will forgive it, come your good fortune. Eh? What?" She started at a soft step behind her.

"Ah, Pilipala, child." Her voice recovered its thoughtful distance. "Our Eilian does not feel well, and this is not the day for aches and frowns. I shall brew a healing tea, and you will take her to the fire and make her comfortable until it is ready."

She drew Pilipala after her into her low-roofed burrow, telling her to rouse the child and take her with her blanket out into the clear air. The single chamber, wide and roomy enough, was still uncomfortably close; dry enough, but stuffy, heavy with the fragrance of the herbs and such that hung in long strings from one of the wooden beams supporting the sod roof. While Pilipala coaxed Eilian from her bed and wrapped her in the blanket, she managed to watch Mamgu from the corner of her eye.

The old woman moved with her lantern among the strings of herbs and dried mushrooms, taking first a few leaves of basil, a common remedy for headache, and mild. Next to it hung, in clumps tied along a single cord, what looked to be betony, lupine, wenwort, yarrow, penny-royal—dwarf dwostle, as some called it—and celandine. Mamgu plucked a leaf or two from each, and from another string half in shadow. Though Pilipala had little herb lore, she wondered at this. But seeing Mamgu's gaze turn toward her, she dropped her own and hurried the protesting Eilian out through the door. Still, it was an odd mixture to be brewing to wake a sleepy child. She remembered some such a mixture being used to *put* Elfodd to sleep the time he had been brought home with his head cracked by a watchman's staff.

Mamgu found her with Eilian cradled beside her, their bare feet warming at the fire. Stooping, the old woman set a shallow bowl on a rock among the coals and, crumbling the leaves into it, half filled it with steaming water from one of the large kettles that hung on the spit. When it had steeped a while and was ready, Eilian was asleep again.

"Here," Mamgu whispered, passing the bowl to Pilipala. "Wake her and see that she drinks all of it." Pushing herself up, she padded over to the table where the dress and the garlands were spread.

Eilian opened her eyes at her friend's urging. They were dark with sleep and with the aching. With an impatient gesture, she pushed the bowl away, spilling a part of it in the ashes at the fire's edge. Only at Pilipala's assurance that the basil and celandine had great virtue as remedies for the headache and even tired eyes would she drink any of it.

"Phh! It's a foul taste." She grimaced, lowering the bowl half emptied.

Mamgu's back was to them. Quickly, Pilipala bent and

94

took a taste of it on her tongue. There was a queer bitterness she could not put a name to, and on an impulse she emptied the remainder of the liquid into the ashes, keeping it clear of the coals, where the hiss and steaming would betray her to Mamgu. The bowl, with its sodden dregs, she set openly beside her.

Afterward, she felt she had been foolish, for Eilian's frown faded, her eyes were clear again, and she was awake, if not alert. She made no protest at Mamgu's fussing over her at the fireside, taking off her old gown, so carefully mended and brightened with ribbons and silk after the cousins' fashion. She stood quietly while her face and neck and arms and feet were washed, dreaming of fresh milk and hot porridge for breakfast. It would be good to be home and living with a cow again, where the milk was not always sour and the butter half rancid. Dreamily, she supposed that it must be because the cousins milked other men's cows in faraway pastures and pinched butter from distant dairies. "Much better to have your own cow." She nodded, speaking aloud.

"Well, yes," murmured Pilipala doubtfully, in surprise, as she slipped the white damask dress over Eilian's upstretched arms.

Plump, kindly Gwladus snorted. "Featherbrain! The child is hungry. Have we left her any porridge? There's no milk, but she can have it with a knob of butter. You'd like that, wouldn't you, love?"

"Yes, please." Eilian raised her arms again, obediently, so that Mamgu could slip a satin stomacher, slightly yellowed but embroidered with tendrils of ivy, around her middle

95

and fasten it. "Why, I've a new gown, haven't I?" she asked, spinning the words out in slow surprise and swinging so that the skirt whirled wide. "It seems very fine for such a long trip, Mamgu. What if it were rained on? What if it were rained on?" she repeated. She plucked the gown up by its hem and stared at her feet in the satin slippers, tied on with ribbons. "Rained on," she said sadly, as if they were already muddied.

Mamgu went on brushing Eilian's red-gold hair down around her shoulders. "You will be safely home before it rains," she promised—rather rashly, Pilipala thought. After all, morning could be clear as clear, and rain might come pelting down at midday. Still, her own unease had nothing to do with the weather. As Gwladus handed the bowl of porridge across, Pilipala passed it to Eilian and walked to her own hole to wrap her few bits and pieces into a bundle. There wasn't much. A handful of soiled ribbons, a few fresh ones, an old blue kirtle, a pair of yellow knitted hose, and a silver bell. Emrys had brought it from Harlech a year ago and slipped it to her in the middle of a dance. She pulled her long hair over her shoulder and, tying the bell onto a ribbon, knotted it among her locks.

A peal of laughter rang out—Eilian's—and Pilipala crept out, alarmed. Mamgu's angry whisper hissed through the dimness like a knife's edge. "Hush you, child! No need to rouse the men. They've their day yet ahead of them. This is ours."

Eilian sat astride a pretty, nervous little pony, her skirts trailing almost to the ground. "The poor love must walk beneath a tent," she had said with the ringing laugh that brought the rebuke. Now she waited, docile and silent,

96

while the others helped Mamgu to mount and hung the remaining garlands around the ponies' necks and their own shoulders. Seeing the child's uncaring calm and sensing in it something worrisome and strange, gentle Pilipala moved close, resting one hand on the pony's rump. At the touch, the pony grew quiet, and the little procession moved past the spring out into the dim foredawn. They followed down the stream to the river, for though the other path was more direct, Mamgu would not set foot in the high wood before the sun was up.

They came along the deepening river from under the wood's eaves just as the sun touched the westward mountaintops and moved through the greening grass as lightly as a summer breeze. Had anyone stood watching on the wood's hill, they would have seemed a procession of the Court of Spring on some antique tapestry, or a painted miniature of the seasons in some old manuscript. The girls went before, garlanded and as brilliant as flowers sown in the vivid grass. Pilipala and another led the ponies, and Mamgu, riding after Eilian, seemed an echo of sky and water in her new blue cloak. The older women came after, singing an old song among themselves. Eilian, Pilipala at her side, was crowned with lilies and willow leaves.

They moved down through the heather and tall grasses, passing the turning that led north onto the foothills, following the river as it spread and deepened. Eilian smiled and nodded, back in her dream of Llwyn Cerddin. The others had left off their singing, bewildered, but Pilipala was filled with dread, for they came, in the first wash of sunlight, to the ford, and no road or way north to the Vale of Conwy lay beyond it. The road that climbed out of the water to skirt the hills opposite joined a grass-grown Roman road a few miles on and cut southward, straight as an arrow's flight.

SEVEN

. . . and the soft nose of a new-foaled pony. The foam of Alis's milk frothing up as the thin stream hissed into the pail. I would like to have a goat when we are rich, Eilian dreamed. It would dance atop the low stone wall by the orchard when it was small and run beneath the ponies' feet on the hillsides. When it was grown it would be easier to milk than Alis. Unless it were a kicker. I shall learn to make cheeses, too.

"You must have a goat, Mamgu," she sang out, swinging her hair and smiling at the sky. "When I am rich, I shall give you a goat, a little goat."

Mamgu nodded, pleased. "Now, there's a good child. A dear child. Yes, you shall give us many good things when you are rich. And," she added craftily, "perhaps even a little room in your great house for your grandmother, with a fine soft bed of goosedown?"

"Oh, I don't know that Mam will want you to live with us." The words slipped out as easily as they were honest. "But I shall give you a wee goat, and a goose if you wish to grow goosefeathers."

The clover in the grass was a drift of white feathers, settling on a rolling green counterpane, greener than Mrs. Price's, and with an embroidered river winding across it, all stitched with blue and with winking gems this was. On both sides the heather hills marched abreast with them. The pony's feet pushed the path along behind, and it seemed they walked and walked and gained no ground. She swayed.

"Cousin, are you ill?"

Pilipala's whisper wakened her from a long fall. Somehow she had been sitting in a treetop trying to pluck a note on a silver harp. Pilipala. Sweet and simple Pilipala. Almost dim. But very dear. She seemed far away walking there at the pony's shoulder.

"No, but I was falling. It's all right, I think."

The track broadened beneath the pony's hoofs and her own dangling slippered feet and then became damp sand and shingle. The cousins milled at the water's edge, looking to Mamgu for what to do. Even those who had come this far, thinking no more deeply than to have a pretty walk and a fond farewell, were doubtful.

"Do we go back and you ride on, Mamgu?"

"Are you sure you've come right, Mamgu?" another asked, thinking only now of the turning they had not taken.

"Yes," said Pilipala, gaining courage. "We cannot fare north by this road."

Mamgu stared ahead as if she watched for someone. "Do you think my wits as weak as that, mistress? We go to a feast first, at Perllan," she added reluctantly, seeing how they held back.

Eilian seemed pleased. At least she smiled in a distant way and reached out to jingle the bell in Pilipala's hair. "Do not frown so, cousin. Perhaps there may be sweetmeats and cakes." She yawned. "And then I shall go home."

Reassured, the others gathered up their skirts and waded into the stream, the ponies following.

"Hai!"

The hail rang out behind them at the same moment the younger cousins, coming up out of the river and onto the grassy roadway, sighted riders far down the South Road, cantering toward them.

"Hai!"

"Emrys!" Pilipala cried, lighting up.

"Don't be a fool, child," Mamgu snapped as she urged her pony past and toward the bank. "Emrys is well on his way to Bala. Don't stand there gawping. Come along."

"No," Pilipala answered suddenly, surprisingly. "No, it's Emrys. And we must be waiting for him."

She pulled at the pony's halter rope and struck him on the rump, forcing him to turn in midstream. Eilian, near drifting off to sleep, was almost unseated in the scramble. She lost her coronet of flowers and leaves to the shallow water, where it floated in a slow, wide swirl until the narrowing, deepening waters below the ford whirled it away.

While Mamgu raged on the other side and the cousins stood whispering behind her back, Emrys appeared on the grassy knoll overlooking the ford. Seeing them, he urged his pony down and through the clover at a dead run. When he came to a plunging stop beside Pilipala, his cheeks were windburned and he was furious.

"Emrys!" Eilian laughed. "What are you doing here? Mamgu said you could not come. Is it that you did not wish to miss the feast?"

Her uncle ignored her and shouted across the broad shallows to Mamgu. "Where do you think you are going? What devil's work is it you are up to? Where did you think to take the child, old woman?"

Mamgu swelled up, red-faced and blustering. "Do you speak to your old mother in such a fashion, Emrys ap Gruffydd? I make no accounting to you, my lad. Your business is in Bala, not here." She cast an uneasy glance over her shoulder. The horsemen were no more than half a mile away and moving briskly. "Get you gone, and I will forget your defiance."

"It won't do. It won't do, Mam." He spoke in a lower tone, but one that still carried to her clearly. "Who may your visitors coming there be? None you wish me to meet, I'll guess."

Mamgu's agitation increased. "You *must* go, Emrys. You will be the ruining of us all."

His anger rose. "Or you'll be the death of us all. Come across now while you can. And while you come, tell the good cousins why you slipped sleeping potions to their men in last evening's wine to keep them fast abed this morning. If you can!"

Pilipala gasped. "Did she, then?"

"Yes," he said grimly, not looking at her but watching the progress of the riders and the confusion that eddied around Mamgu. "Do you know, I killed the little mare. She ran till her sweet heart stopped, just inside the wood. So I came by the dingle to find another mount, and they were all asleep, even the watcher at his post. Elis came around after I pushed his head in the spring. He and the others will be coming as soon as they've found their wits. What has she done to our Eilian here?"

"It was a sleeping draft, but with something strange in it, I think. She's been all smiles and dreams."

"Into the cruel hawk's mouth," he muttered. Then, cupping his hands to his mouth, he called, "I am taking the child back. I'll wait no longer."

The cousins, torn between obedience to Mamgu and their fear at seeing that the riders were so many, and some of them armed, wavered. A few at first, and then all of them, deserted Mamgu, splashing back the way they had come.

"Come back, you sheep," she shrieked. "You're in no danger. It's your fortunes we are making."

And then she saw her kinsmen and their sons, afoot, running down through the flowery field and the women running to meet them. Terrified at last, she wheeled her pony into the water, but it stopped there, trembling, and would not go on. Behind, the riders gave a shout and lashed their horses into a gallop, as if the men in the field were game to be chased. Two of the riders were gentlemen, and the other five were dressed as servants, but wore swords, as their masters did. One of the gentlemen laughed shrilly and drew his sword. Emrys' heart tightened, for he and his cousins carried no more than knives.

"Come, Mam, come away!" He urged his pony toward the old woman, who sat astride hers in midstream, weeping with rage and helplessness. "You're safe if you can make the wood. Ah, Mam, what is it you have done to us?"

With Emrys' coming, Eilian, who had ridden since dawn

in a waking slumber, had been roused from her uncaring, drifting dreaming to what seemed a nightmarish confusion of shouts and clattering hoofs. Why did Mamgu wrangle with Emrys as he pulled her pony along? Why did . . .

Then, for the first time, she saw the riders clearly. Racing in front was a young man—little more than a boy—richly dressed, whose black felt hat wore a curling cockade of red and white feathers she had seen before.

"Simon. Simon Rastall," she whispered, and both Emrys and Pilipala saw her face, though neither heard the words.

"Run, Pilipala! Get her safe away to the wood," he commanded. "Scatter!" he shouted to the others.

The Red Fairies fled, blown like bright petals up the green slopes.

With Emrys' command, Pilipala wavered no longer. She dropped her bundle and, swinging a hard slap to the pony's shoulder, headed Eilian's mount up the long valley. Running as if her feet were winged, she kept pace and twisted her fingers in the pony's mane. They fairly flew. Eilian, craning to look back over her shoulder, could see one of the servingmen pounding behind, and the others fanning out to the east. Ahead, one last bright dress flickered out of sight in the taller grass, hidden by a rise from the pursuers below. A second horseman veered in their direction.

"It's the gown," Eilian cried in Pilipala's ear. "That Simon's seen the white gown. What is over yonder? Can we go that way?" She pointed to their left as they topped the rise. They veered sharply once out of sight, but about fifty yards farther on, the ground fell away steeply. The sound of rushing water rose to them.

"Not here. Above," Pilipala gasped. Saving her breath,

she made a sign to show that the river ran below, spilling down a series of rock falls. "Stream divides above. Upper ford," she panted.

They came to an outcropping of stone—almost a pillar of rock—and slowed, angling down the slope toward the water. A smaller stream, flowing down from the western foothills, joined the river, and above this point they found a place to cross. Because of the unevenness of the ground Eilian could not see whether they had lost the two horsemen. The sound of the water covered the sound of hoofbeats, her own pony's as well. Slowing to a walk, Pilipala coaxed the animal forward along the north side of the smaller stream, sliding here, stepping carefully there, until they were walking at the water's edge in a deep cut, the hills rising on both sides. Gradually the cut widened, the little river ran more quietly, and the hills were less steep. Stopping, they could hear faint shouts in the distance.

"They are far to the east," Pilipala said. "The cousins have lured them that way so that they will not find the dingle. We can leave the stream now. Even if they saw us, they could not follow before we reached the wood. And they will not venture very far beyond its borders when there are so few of them."

At the brow of the hill, Eilian saw that they stood at the southern end of the foothills bordering the western wood. It was not far from the place where she had first met the Red Fairies, coming like fireflies on the dark hill. To the south, the grasslands rolling down toward the wide river seemed empty, though once or twice there was a distant cry.

They were halfway to the wood when a ringing of hoof

on stone stopped them. It came from behind; the way they had come. Quickly, Eilian slipped down and, whispering coaxing noises to the pony, pulled it down to lie in the high grass beside them.

"It sounds a pony, not a horse," Pilipala whispered, ear to the ground. Then she froze. A second set of hoofbeats echoed lightly but sharply after the first. The pony between the two girls raised its head and nickered softly. An answering snort came from close at hand, and then a familiar whistle.

"Goronwy?" Eilian leaped up and went to meet him, her own pony following. Pilipala sat, not moving, in the grass.

"It's all right, cousin," Eilian explained. "He is my friend. From home."

"How do you, poetess?" The grave smile of greeting he gave Eilian seemed out of some other world than the wild one she was fleeing in.

"Well enough, but very confused," she answered. "It seems everyone is upside down because of me. I can't sort it all out."

"Time enough for that later," he said. "The both of you must come into the wood before one of Rastall's men thinks to come this way." He unfastened his cloak and put it around her shoulders, hiding the white gown. "The night-ingale must keep free of the hawk's mouth."

Pilipala was wide-eyed, bewildered again, and would not come. Goronwy's words recalled the phrase she had heard Emrys mutter, but this only deepened her alarm. Rising and turning as if to run, she saw the pony that had followed them. It came to her, sides and neck dark with sweat from the running, and rubbed its muzzle in her hand. For a moment she did not move, and Eilian and Goronwy wondered at it. But when she turned, her face still and unafraid, Eilian knew.

"It's Emrys' pony, Eilian. You'd best go quickly to the wood. I must go back."

She mounted quickly. They watched her out of sight over the brow of the hill, retracing their steps from the river branch.

Eilian would go no farther than the borders of the wood. At first, fearing for Emrys, she had wished to follow Pilipala, but Goronwy prevented her. "Your uncle would not thank you for undoing the good he has won at such risk," he said. But he understood her anxiety and shared it.

"If we move eastward toward the river, I know a tree tall enough to give me a view down toward the South Fork and the road," he offered.

He gave Eilian a hand up onto his own pony and, turning to the nervous little beast she had ridden, spoke gently to it and sent it south across the slopes. "It will come to its home pasture in time," he said.

They moved in the shadows at the wood's edge, keeping a screen of trees between them and the heather slopes outside. Here they could move quietly, for though the ground was uneven, it was earth, not stone. Patches of thin grass grew where the sun had reached on early spring mornings. They followed no path but wound among low shrubs and thickets, where stunted young white beams and quickbeams struggled with each other for what thin sunlight came to them. They came to one of the Red Fairies' paths and crossed it warily. At length they came to a crest overlooking the running stream below. Here and on the hill that fell away toward the water, the trees were of thicker girth, and taller, and little sunlight could pass through their leaves. Some were shaggy ancient trees that climbed downward, their great roots reaching, grasping, binding them to the hillside or anchoring them along the bank where they trailed their branches in the water. The river there was narrow but swift.

On the high ground, Goronwy led his pony into a stand of slender young birch trees and helped Eilian to alight. "Sit still here, and I will be back in a moment."

She saw him gesture toward a great lone elm tree that stood in shadow beyond a fall of sunlight. From its girth she judged it must be well over a hundred feet tall. It was almost as if it had been planted, long ages ago, to be a sentinel to the wood. Eilian could not imagine how Goronwy meant to climb it. The lowest branch was more than twenty feet above the ground. Even the birches grew tall here. To her amazement, he turned, touched the birch trunk lightly, as if to measure the height of a branch a good fifteen feet up, drew back, and took a half run, half leap that carried him high enough to catch the branch and swing himself nimbly up onto it. From high in the birches, he leaped into the elm and was gone from sight.

Her astonishment for a moment drove away her fear for Emrys and her sickness at heart from Mamgu's treachery. She had not really taken Emrys seriously when he accused Goronwy of being other than he wished to seem. But such a leap! She wondered at it, thinking that no man could manage such a feat. But if he were something more. . . . She shivered, drawing the cloak around her. The wool as she touched it seemed silken smooth and, she noticed, was

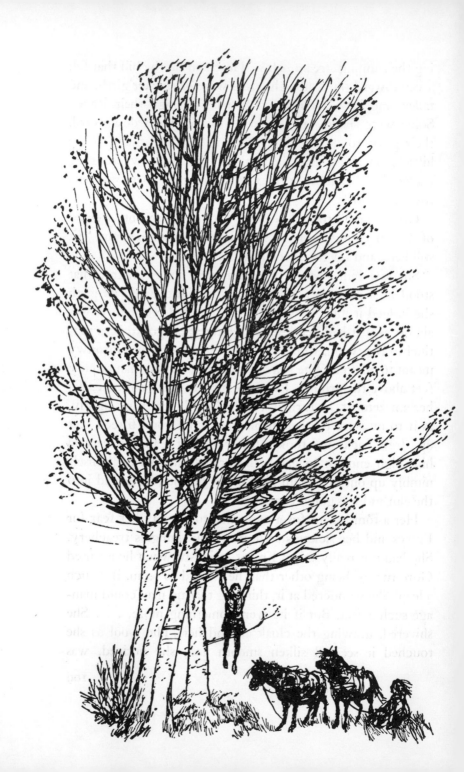

rough beneath her fingers only when she stroked it upward, as if that were against the grain. Lifting a fold, she looked at it more sharply and found it was not woolen stuff, for all its warmth. There was a queer iridescence to it, and there was neither pattern nor visible line where gray-green darkened or melted into a rose-brown.

"No, it cannot *be*," she said, half aloud. Goronwy came from the hills above home, not this legend-haunted forest. Glancing up, she caught the pony's eye, and it seemed to contemplate her altogether too wisely for comfort. He wore neither bridle nor halter nor rope. She remembered that he needed only a touch or a whistle, no other command. More, Goronwy had spoken of kinfolk not far away. Desperately, she did not wish it to be so. Once—it seemed so long ago—when she had been dreading a world of gloves and fine needlework and ladylike cakes and tea, to be one of the Red Fairies had seemed the furthest reach of freedom. But always they were her own blood and had seemed no more or less than human even at their most magical. And even at their least they were not frightening. Except, perhaps, Mamgu, she amended. The Fair Folk, though . . . men feared and hated them and dared not refuse their demands, for they were . . . not human. Some whispered that they were demons. If Goronwy were not human . . .

She stared upward at the roof of leaves. The trees were hung in patches with old leaves, yellowed and dry, as well as with the fresh and rustling green. While she watched, Goronwy came swinging down to drop feet-first on the grass. He came to kneel beside her, clearly worried.

"The riders have gone," he said. "I saw them riding in a

knot along the South Road and watched them out of sight."

"But that is miles away," she protested, seeing the clearness of his gray eyes.

He looked at her quizzically. "I am farsighted," he said briefly. "Your grandmother must be safe away. At least, I saw no blue cloak upon the hill. And though there are dips and swells enough to hide a pony from view, the birds and rabbits moved as if the falling valley were all their own again."

"And . . . Emrys and Pilipala?"

He frowned. "I do not know. The ford itself was hidden from my view, but something has happened there. I am sure of it. I will see you safe, I think, and then ride down to see."

"Not to the Red Fairies' dingle!" She scrambled up and held her hand out to him. "You will not make me go there?"

"No," he said slowly, "for I think your uncle would not wish it. Do you remember the stream where he came upon us talking? That is north of here, perhaps a mile. I will take you there and then make my way down the foothills to the fords."

Eilian had lost all count of time, but soon after Goronwy's leaving, her stomach began to tell her it had been too many hours since the warmed-over porridge she had made a breakfast of. Yet to stop and think, it seemed even longer past, a world almost forgotten. The bewilderment and anger returned. Deceitful snare of a world. How *could* they sell her to the Rastalls? She could think of no other explanation for it. Her heart was like a stone when she thought of them.

On her knees by the stream, she cupped her hands and drew some water up to drink. It was clear, cold, and refreshing. She drank her fill and then stood to look around her. There would be no berries where there were no bushes, but with luck she might find something. Taking care to keep the sound of the brook in hearing, she explored downstream for a considerable distance and found nothing, not even a sweet grass to chew on. She saw a series of fleshy gray shelflike fungi climbing a dead birch trunk, but they were of a kind too tough and corky to be edible. Upstream, kicking through the dead leaves underfoot, she came upon first one mushroom of a beautiful bluish green and then two more. They had the strong, fragrant smell of aniseed, and though she had not thought to find them in a mountain forest, she knew them for what Mam called "Green Aromatics." Washed and cleaned, they made a scant lunch. As time went on, she grew nervous, imagining sounds and steps and fearing for her uncle and friends. What was she to do if they did not appear before nightfall?

They came at last, in the late afternoon, through the deepening shadows. At first they were only a slow rustling in the dead leaves, a fearsome sound, but soon a fold of Pilipala's bright gown flickered in the distance, and Eilian ran to meet her, scarcely limping. Goronwy was afoot, and as he walked, he steadied Pilipala, who rode beside him, deathly weary, supporting Emrys before her.

"Talk can wait," said Goronwy when he saw the questions trembling on Eilian's tongue. "He is sorely hurt, and not even your Mamgu with all her leechdoms and herb-cunning can help him now. You have no choice but to forget your fears and to come into the heart of the Dark Wood. There is one there who may be able to heal him."

EIGHT

"From what little she said that I could make any sense of," Pilipala said, "Mamgu thought she could bribe the law, through the Squire, to keep clear of the Wood. And she thought that once you were a great lady, you would forgive her and protect us all. She would not believe what Emrys said of your danger. Did she never know of Simon's cruelty to you, then? No more than we?"

"No, I suppose not," Eilian admitted. "I told it only that once, to Mam and Dad. It may be that Mamgu knew no more than that Sir Edmund coveted Plaseirian. Here, is this enough?" She held out a wide strip of damask torn from the front of her skirt.

Pilipala folded it into a square. Emrys' head and shoulders lay in her lap, and she bent over, reaching inside the wide rent Goronwy had made in the tunic to slip the pad under the makeshift bandage.

"He is so pale," she faltered. "We oughtn't have come so far when the dingle was near."

Eilian said, "Goronwy promised he would not be long coming with help. It was the riding so awkwardly over rough ground that did the harm." She pulled Goronwy's cloak up to cover her uncle. It was only early evening in the outside world, but they had come into a pine wood so deep and black that it seemed almost as dark and cold as middle-night.

Pilipala shivered. "Poor Mamgu. She grudged to give up her grand plan for marrying you—and all the rest of us with you—into Squire Rastall's wealth. She grudged it despite her fearing that Emrys and the others would be taken as thieves under her nose. She had plotted to keep them away for fear the Overseers might catch wind of something and try to ambush and arrest them. Even after Emrys roused the men from the dingle and came for us, I think she was so convinced of the Squire's goodwill that she hoped to talk them free. Elis says she turned back to the ford, where the other young gentleman waited, with Emrys racing after her. It was there that the other came up behind."

"That Simon." Eilian covered her face. "That stinking pig of a Simon. No one else could be so cowardly! Ah, if only I had known it was *his* father who was your Squire of Perllan! And the smirk on Simon-Pig's face when he saw that I knew him!"

"Hush, hush," crooned Pilipala sadly. "Mamgu said enough of that for us all. And it was his father's doing in the end. Not his own."

Eilian looked up, startled. "How do you mean?"

The young man at the ford, Eilian supposed as she heard the tale, must have been Simon's cousin Fabian. Some stirring of compassion had prompted him to call out, "Turn back, old woman. The girl's away, and Sir Edmund will think it your treachery!" but Simon had heard him and came pelting down across the field. The ponies were no match for the high-blooded horse he rode, and he came quickly up behind them, sword in hand. Emrys fell without a word, without even seeing his attacker. Elis had seen all this from above and saw the servingmen answer Simon's call, converging on the ford. Yet though they circled the old woman, taunting her, they did not offer her any harm. Sir Edmund may have given orders that the woman be spared, but it was more as if they half feared her and did not dare to seize her.

She knelt in the grass, crooning over her son, rocking back and forth, not hearing the taunts. Elis had not understood what was happening when she bent low and the rocking stopped, but after a moment he saw her rise with a wild shriek of "Treachery, treachery!" that echoed up the hill. A white paper fluttered in her hand. Then she had poured out a torrent of words he could not hear. The riders drew back, edging their horses into the water. They had sheathed their swords and backed away, to splash across the ford and turn down the South Road at a pace that seemed almost as if they fled.

"Elis and I met on the hillside and went down," Pilipala recounted. "We thought Emrys dead, he lay so still. Elis put Mamgu on his pony—her own was gone. She was like a child, obeying him, but she kept repeating wildly, 'The Red Fairies' curse be on your head. May your father see you at his feet so!' Elis would have me go with them, but I could not. After a while your friend came."

"You said it was Simon's father's doing. How did Mamgu know that?"

"From this. The letter Emrys was taking to Bala." Pilipala reached inside her bodice and brought out the folded
paper, wrinkled and stained. "Can you read it to me?"

Eilian unfolded it and held it close. In the darkness she
could make out the writing only with difficulty:

For Sir Myles Tuder at Afon House.
Sir Myles.

You have ever been forwarde in taking paynes to ad-
vance my pryvat interest, and now I put you in the waye

of substanciall returne. Give this ffellowe in charge to your gaoler Myddelton and see he bee well shacklyd so that he may wait the pleasure of the Chiefe Justice of Assize without fayle. I wold be pleased with no thinge more than a speedy tryall, for he is chiefe of those theffs callyd Red Fayries by the silly simple folke.

Given under my hande
this twent[th] Maye.

Edm. Rastall

Eilian looked up from the paper, her thin face set and cold. Pilipala was a pale shadow opposite, stroking Emrys' forehead. "And you say 'Poor Mamgu'?" Eilian protested. "You should hate her! She bought their treachery with her own, but it is you and Emrys who pay."

"Perhaps." Pilipala sighed. "I only know I would not be in her place for the world. That must be the worst of pains, to know your folly too late and so bitterly."

They sat together in silence, and slowly, reluctantly, Eilian wondered if Pilipala was more right in her simplicity. She was not, like most of the others, an instrument to be played on by the wind, swept into wild words by a moment's anger. Only touch her, and she rang true. There was no separating feeling and action. She simply was. And Eilian had mistaken it for a sweet dimness once.

When Goronwy came, he carried a lamp, and two young men rode behind him. One bore two long staves rolled in what looked to be a rug. Once dismounted, the young men proved taller than Goronwy by an inch or two and looked to be older, but it would have been difficult to know by how many years. They moved—if that was possible—more quickly and surely and did not look to Goronwy for direction. Like him, they were slender, dark, and gray-eyed, but somehow frighteningly fair.

"These are my kinsmen Aratros and Relynos," he said quietly.

They nodded, looking at the girls with a brief curiosity, and then moved to their task. The staves unrolled turned out to be laced to a narrow rug, making a litter on which a man could be carried. They laid it flat on the ground beside Pilipala and with Goronwy's help lifted Emrys gently onto it. Pilipala covered him again with the cloak and stood aside as Aratros and Relynos moved to take up the poles at each end. Neither of the girls had seen such a litter before and were relieved to find it broad enough, and secure. Goronwy brought the ponies forward and, having given each of the girls a hand up, leaped upon his own and went ahead with the lantern. His kinsmen followed, running smoothly, the litter swaying gently between them.

Pilipala and Eilian brought up the rear. Though they could not see their way, it made no matter, for the ponies followed on their own, making no misstep even though the lantern's circle of light fell short of them. From the silence of their going and the sweet pungence of the air, Eilian knew that they still rode through pines. The forest floor was carpeted with long years of needles. After a time they slowed slightly, descending a long, even slope. The sound of swift-running water told that they had come back to the river itself, somewhere well above the dingle. In a while the ring of hoofs on rock spoke of a thinning of the trees overhead. They rode on in a dim twilight.

The stream ran in a gorge some fifteen or twenty feet

119

below—and swiftly, for in its higher reaches it plunged down a long series of falls until here it became a roiling race. The high bank was smooth enough going, though it climbed steadily above the river, but at each of the falls there was a circling path or easy stair, which slowed their progress to a walk. All along the way, rank upon rank of pines and straight, long-limbed firs covered the steep hill on their left. Willows, many stunted by the endless shade, grew along the bank, climbing down to the water. In some places near the falls, one or two had seen enough of the sun to grow thick and heavy, wide-limbed and long-rooted, arching over the stream and the stony banks. Goronwy held the long branches up so that the others could pass under, and then took the lead again. They left no trail even a skilled woodsman could follow, despite their haste. The way was all pine needles or rock, and the ponies left no mark, being lightfooted and unshod.

At length the walls of the river valley closed in so narrowly and steeply that no trees kept footholds on the slopes. The hills became sheer rock faces peopled by the lantern's light with looming shadows of the small company. The way was narrow but smooth, and they moved quickly. Eilian thought several times she heard a whistle high in the air but, looking up, saw only the dark fringe of trees that topped the looming cliffs. Gradually, she realized that they were no longer climbing. The hills dropped away into the dusk, the river swung away from them, and they moved down along a path through a high-vaulted grove of beeches and oaks and birches. The white trunks of the birches gleamed in the moving light and seemed almost to mark their way, an avenue through the wood.

Abruptly, the river reappeared before them. But it seemed two rivers running side by side, for a grassy tongue of land ran down between the two channels. Lights danced along it, glowing in the grass like green jewels.

"We must cross here. We are a way above the waters-meet, and the stream is broadest and smoothest here," said Goronwy, riding back to the girls.

Pilipala slipped from her mount and ran forward to the river's edge, where the young men stood with the litter, waiting the shadowy boat that slid across from the opposite shore. Goronwy came after, with the lamp. Pilipala saw the flush that had risen in Emrys' cheeks even before she touched his forehead and felt its burning. He moaned, dreaming in his fever, and Eilian saw Aratros and Goronwy exchange glances, and her heart quailed.

The shadow-boat scraped against the bank, and a cloaked figure leaped out to secure it by a rope to a ring set there in a large rock for that purpose. With the other oarsman he helped to steady the broad, shallow-bottomed boat while the litter was lifted aboard and laid like a hammock between the thwarts at front and back. Pilipala leaped in after and sat beside Emrys on a cushion one of the oarsmen brought from beneath his seat. Taking Emrys' hand, she shut all else from her mind, for the strangeness of the dark journey and coming among the Children—for though none had ever seen them, she, unlike Eilian, had never doubted their presence in the wood's heart—all this was too much to bear beside her worry. Fear and wonder could wait for the morrow. And so nothing of the river crossing and the passing through field and orchard into the lamplit gardens of Gardd Terfynol amazed her.

Not so Eilian. She forgot everyone and everything but her wonder from the moment the boat returned and she and Goronwy led the ponies into it. She had never seen such a boat. It was shaped much like the ferry of Caven Gronaunt, which plied across the Conwy, but there the resemblance ended. It was smaller, the wood was polished, and the whole of such fine workmanship that there was not a seam to be seen. The cushions gleamed blue and green in the lantern's light and felt to the touch like the stuff of Goronwy's cloak. When they mounted to ride up through the rushes onto the narrow meadow between the rivers, a last high cloud passed to let fall the first starlight. Riding into the orchards, Eilian saw the starlight shine through thick masses of blossoming pear and apple, lighting the drifting petals and the winding path as a snowy landscape in a dream. In the swinging glow of the lamp, scarlet flowers flamed in the grass. She did not notice that the others had gone ahead without waiting for the boat's return. Under the weight of the orchard's half-seen beauty, her heart bloomed, itself a blood-red flower, until its fullness throbbed in her ears and she swayed.

Goronwy reached out to touch her hand. She was like a babe before it walks, whose wide eyes think stars are flowers hanging in a tree, who overreaches for them and tumbles into grieving. She was a harp played by the moment's wind after all, he thought, and it surprised him that he should feel this such a bitter thing.

"Do you know where you are?" He could not keep a faint coldness from his voice.

Eilian turned toward him. Only slowly, as if he had spoken from a great distance, did she hear the question.

"No," she answered. "For a moment I almost thought I had died. Is it that this is the same wood, the same world?" She marveled.

"Aye, no other. These are trees and that grass, and those, those are flowers."

There was a pause while they rode in silence.

"You are angry. Why are you angry with me?"

He was startled. "Angry? How am I so? Anger is an answer to foes and to defiance."

"What *is* it then? Is it you are teasing me? Have I said something stupid?"

"No, no." He wished he had held his tongue and was uncertain why he had not. "Look you, this is Gardd Terfynol—the Last Garden, as our folk call it. Come. Here we take the turning to the right, to the ash grove at the valley's eastern border. Túdual's house is there."

"And Emrys? Is that where he has been taken?" The remembering came with a rush. She had almost forgotten their reason for coming. It was good that Goronwy could not see her face, she thought, for she felt it flushed with dismay. How unfeeling he must think her! "Can we hurry?" she asked, ashamed.

With a whistle he urged the ponies on, and shortly they came through a wood of large trees widely spaced, to a narrow metaled road. At its end a cluster of lights shone, and those nearest lit a wooden bridge arching over a small brook. The house beyond was unlike any Eilian had seen. It stood off the ground on four legs and was built from the same hard and gleaming wood as the river boat. Each of the legs was a section of a massive tree trunk, and though the roof itself was steeply pitched, the house's heavy eaves thrust out widely so that the roof also afforded cover to a broad walkway, or gallery, around the outer walls. Lamps hung from the eaves' ends and from brackets on the door-posts.

"Come, children, but quietly."

Relynos stood in the doorway and beckoned, a shadow against the light inside. A dark figure came from under the trees to take the ponies.

Eilian hesitated on the gleaming stair. "It's no more than a house and a stair," she told herself fiercely, remembering Goronwy's rebuke. Her hand on the carved rail felt only a much-handled and polished wood. "It's only that," she thought. "It is real enough."

Inside, they were taken through a large hall brightly lit by fire and lamp into another, darker room, where Emrys lay on a curtained bed in an alcove. An old man stood at the bedside, and when he turned, Eilian forgot her fear. She could not think why. He was as strangely beautiful as the others she had seen. His hair was silvered white, and though his clean-shaven face was pale and uncannily beautiful, his eyes were blue and kindly. He was dressed severely, in a long gray tunic bordered at the hem with blue.

"And this is the Song-Child? They are very like indeed." This he said to Goronwy, and Eilian took it to mean herself and Emrys and Pilipala. "Come, my dear, be assured. If medicine and lore and quiet have any virtue, your uncle will be safe. I have given him a draft which brings sleep, abates the soreness, and subdues the deeper pain. Yet he is so weak with the fever that I could chance only a small shred of the mandragora rind steeped in the wine. The difficulty has been to stanch the wound, for he has been restless. Still,

I think I have succeeded now." He touched a red jasper stone on a fine chain, which had been put around Emrys' neck, the stone resting on the bandages. "He is young and has been strong, and so I think it hopeful."

Eilian had not thought of her uncle as young. He was twice her own age. Túdual's words made her see him afresh, young and helpless in his fever. I only let him be Uncle, she thought, not Emrys. That was as bad as Mamgu's not letting him be more than he was to her. But now he was his own, and in peril for it. Why, he was almost as much a stranger as Goronwy. It was a queer thought.

"Goronwy, take Eilian to her cousin and see that she has some refreshment. I stay the night here to watch." Túdual drew the curtains around the bed and, pulling an armchair close, made himself comfortable.

In a room off the great hall, a small bower hung with fine woven draperies in blue and green, they found Pilipala sitting on a low couch, half asleep herself. Lamps hung from the beamed ceiling, and shelves in curious niches were piled with books and skeins of brightly dyed yarns. In one corner a loom stood, and in another a second couch. On a low table had been set cups and a flagon, plates of small cakes made of rye and honey, and, in a bowl carved from a single green stone, nuts and sweetmeats.

"Emrys? Is he sleeping still?" Pilipala roused herself.

"Yes. And he is looking better. Truly he is." Eilian lied hopefully.

Goronwy spoke from the doorway. "You are to sleep here and not to worry. Aratros and Relynos and I will sleep in the hall."

"Will the physician call me if Emrys wakes?" Pilipala asked.

"Yes, of course. But he is a lord as well as sage and physician. And it is his will that you eat now and rest." Stepping back, he drew a heavy curtain across the doorway.

"Have you noticed?" Eilian whispered to Pilipala. "There are no doors. None at all. What do you make of this place?"

"It is strange," Pilipala answered simply.

After they had eaten, Eilian blew out the lamps and drew the soft draperies along the far wall, opening the room onto the moonlit gardens. The gallery passed under the low parapet at her feet, and halfway down its length she heard low voices murmuring by the stair. After a while they went away, and she groped to find her way to the far couch. Despite the questions that tumbled in her head, she was asleep in minutes.

NINE

"Slug-a-beds! Come, you must be stirring." There was laughter in Goronwy's voice when he saw them curled together atop the coverlets like mice in a nest. Hanging in at the window, one knee on the parapet, he twitched the bedclothes sharply.

"Come, there's a messenger come from the Lord and Lady to be having a look at you."

Eilian sat up and rubbed at her eyes. The draperies at the wide window rippled in a cool breeze, but there was no morning chill in the room. Outside, Goronwy smiled, and the sun stood high above the gardens.

"How long have we slept?" She yawned and stretched.

"Almost into noon. Here, I have brought you milk and bread and honey to breakfast on."

"Pilipala?" Eilian nudged at her. "Cousin? Goronwy says the day's half gone. Yes, it was no dream," she said when the older girl opened her eyes to stare uncomprehendingly at the room.

There were dark shadows under Pilipala's eyes, smudges that spoke of weariness and a restless night. "I feel I only now put my head down," she said. "Is . . ."

"Túdual reports our friend to be resting more easily; that the fever is fallen." Goronwy answered the unspoken question.

Pilipala swung her feet to the floor and found a pair of slippers standing ready.

"There are gowns on the chair." Goronwy pointed. "The Lady sent them. I'll return after you've dressed, to be helping you eat up all this food." He reached up and drew the shimmering curtains between them.

The gowns were both of a green stuff softer than taffeta but with a similar sheen. There were undergarments and blue petticoats as well, and even ribbons for Pilipala's hair, a silver comb, and a silver-backed mirror made of a flat disk of polished green stone.

After they had dressed in the new gowns, Eilian answered a dozen questions about the house, the folk, the gardens with "I don't know" until Pilipala at last gave it up and set to pulling the soiled and stringy ribbons from her hair. She saved only the bit that held the silver bell. Eilian offered to comb and braid her long hair, and worked swiftly, twining blue ribbons and red-gold hair.

"I wish mine will be like yours one day, cousin."

"Your hair? Much nicer, if you are not cutting it. For yours is fairer, look you."

She pulled a strand of Eilian's near her own. Though the light in the room was dimmed by the curtains, Eilian's did seem less red, more golden.

"It is, yes. Only see now till I . . . there, your bell's on!" Eilian limped to the window and drew the draperies. "Come, breakfast."

Pilipala pulled on the new slippers. "After I've seen Emrys." She slipped out through the doorway.

Eilian sat on the parapet licking honey from her fingers and thinking. Goronwy had been very cheerful considering last evening's sourness. Perhaps it was this valley. Who could be sour or unkind in such a place? In the gardens below the gallery, masses of flowers bloomed, laburnum trees were heavy with golden chains of blossoms, and the wood beyond was more like the park of some great palace than a forest. Beyond the ash grove, many kinds of trees, huge and ancient, stood each to itself in dignity, the meadow lapping around them. Along the brook, above the bridge, great weeping willows trailed beside the laburnums, and flowers bloomed in the long grass. The only stirring was a few small butterflies. Not a soul was in sight.

"How lovely to be here always," she thought. "To sit singing in the grass and learn the harping." Her fingers plucked the air as she had seen Emrys finger his harp. "And they were never heard of again," she whispered. Of course, Emrys and Pilipala might not wish to stay, but how could they go when the world outside waited to eat them up? Still, there was Dad and Mam. Were they ever to hear of her again? For the first time she felt a sharp pain, one the peace and beauty could not soothe, and it left her both frightened and confused. It was not the sadness at the loss of Dad's kindness, as it had been before. It was a sense of his fearing and Mam's anguish, for Mam would be beginning to doubt that her folk had turned to honest farming and would be following a thread of thought that led from her lost child to. . . . Why, Mam would be frantic, for all her grudging. To fear you'd lost a child. . . . It was no wonder then that folk who thought they had a changeling worried so. It was for the other child, the one they'd not be hearing of again.

She began to sing quietly and then, as the thought moved her, raised the unrhymed chant to ring the wood full of silver sound.

"When we went out among the roses
    To the gate,
  It was but coming seven,
    And the western sun
Sheeted the cornfields in ashen gold,
    Edged by dark
That grew in ragged hedgerows
    And the gold-crowned wood.

The pale road drew us past
    The open farmyard gate
And wound south, woven to the way's edge
    By garlands
Of azaleas, some white,
    Some crimson in the dusk,
The unwatched house behind us,
    Screened by arching leaves.
We heard soft rustling steps,
    A singing in the wood,
High sweet laughter, and—
    Half afraid, dismayed—turned back.

We had no business to be out.
    Once through the gate
And the welcome door
    We sat down to ale and cheese,
Joking that the baby
    Might be a changeling now—
Smiling at ourselves
    And hiding the bone-deep fear."

As the notes fell away, she turned to see Goronwy, somber again, standing near the stair with a dark person wrapped in a dove-gray cloak. The visitor bowed, said something to the boy, and went down the stair to where his pony was tethered. Goronwy came, sat down, and dipped a piece of bread in the honeypot.

"Was that the messenger you said had come? What was it he wanted?"

"To have a look at the three of you. And bid Mistress Eilian come to the . . . well, I suppose you would call it 'the village.' "

"Only me? Not Pilipala?"

"She will not come. I think they knew she would not. Your uncle sleeps yet." He ate the piece of bread slowly, then licked his fingers. "Tell me, do you feel about us as you sang?"

"How is it you are meaning?"

" 'The bone-deep fear'?"

"I was singing about others' fear. But yes, I, too. A little," she admitted.

He was quiet.

She faltered, not knowing how to put her questions. "I do not understand how you can be so like and yet so unlike us."

"That's only me." He grinned ruefully, reluctantly. "My mother's father was a mortal man. It's why I am unreliable, Túdual says. Because I do not distrust or fear you as I should."

"Fear *me?*" She was astonished.

He stared at the lovely garden, unseeing. "The Children have a legend. They will not tell me it. But when they heard of your coming to the dingle, I was forbidden to speak with you. It has something to do with their old tale, I think."

"Goronwy?"

"Yes?"

"Why were you angry with me last evening?"

"Because I am mad." He shrugged. "No, because you had shut out all the world except the beauty. You were living in your eyes."

"That doesn't make sense. Does it? Wasn't it because I forgot Emrys? I was sorry after. But," she said hopefully, "isn't that what the Fair Family do? Live without pain in riches and beauty?"

"Is it?"

"*Isn't* it? Look you, it is what I have always wished for. I shall be getting over the fearing. If only . . ."

She felt the twinge again. Mam and Dad.

"If only?"

"Nothing."

"Ah, well. It's very good voice you are in. Perhaps they will be keeping you for a singing bird," he quipped. "Despite their fearing you."

" 'They'?"

"Aye, not I. They will be wishing now they'd sent me home the day I came. I am to go as soon as all's decided."

"I thought you would be . . . stopping here." She was suddenly uncertain.

"No," he said simply. "Come, if we set out walking now, we will come to the village at the hour the Lord and Lady bade us appear."

He helped her over the sill, and they went along the gallery to the stair. At the bridge Eilian pulled back.

"Where are the ponies? Why can we not ride?"

"Because we need not. Unless you are about to go dead lame."

"No." She smothered a hiccupish laugh. "But I would be fresher for greeting your Lady, not all red and drooping."

"But if you were all red and drooping? With grass stains on your slippers, and bringing flowers?"

Eilian eyed him shrewdly. "I would have 'lived' my way across the garden instead of 'looking' it?"

"Got it in one!"

"Come, I must catch my breath at least."

They had nearly reached the northern side of the valley and stood in a low meadow where there were here and there wych elms, sycamores, and black poplars—even walnut trees, and sweet chestnuts hung thickly with their catkins—among the yews and oaks. From where they stood, the ground rose slightly to the northward, so that Eilian could not see the "village" Goronwy said was just beyond.

"How ever can such trees grow so high upon the mountains?" She marveled.

"All our kind love trees," he said. "Each time we move, we carry seeds with us, and these were planted long ago. The valley faces south and traps the sun, or they would not have done so well."

Eilian pushed the worrisome "our kind" resolutely from her mind. She leaned back against a tree trunk. "I feel I could grow into the tree, I feel the treeness so."

"Not into it, but with it," Goronwy suggested. "To be you and still to feel the otherness so richly—that is a special joy."

134

The trees farther along did not give way to a clearing as Eilian had half expected. The rising ground leveled once more, and she saw directly ahead an oak-clad hill rising up, loaf-shaped, with others, smaller, near it.

"These are the hills of my kinsmen, and Castell Witonos is on their other side. In your tongue that would be Caer Gwydion."

"Caer *Gwydion?*" She stopped almost in midstep, but Goronwy took her hand and drew her on. She went reluctantly, for like all the north country, she knew Gwydion's name and feared it. King of all the Fair Folk in the north, the old wives' tales said he was.

As they passed between the hills, Eilian was amazed to see a doorway into each, with door, posts, and lintels of wood carved with the grain and bound with straps and hinges of a dull metal something like silver. But she had no time to look more closely or to ask if these were burrows like Mamgu's, only finer. Beyond, a great crowd had gathered within a wide arc of birch trees, and lined the path that led to Castell Witonos, a heap of stones against a towering rock wall. This, she thought, was why she had seen no one all the morning.

There must have been hundreds of them, and though most were tall and dark, some were short and brown with open, curious faces. Yet all of these were as disquietingly fair of face as the few maidens with long black hair wavy as waterfalls under the moon's light. Most were simply dressed in blue or green, with few ornaments, but altogether in its shifting murmur the crowd was a richer sight than a peacock's tail. Eilian was a little frightened and much bewildered by the stares and whispers, and took hold of Goronwy's hand.

135

The great heap of stones looked at first to be a fall of rock from the high wall above that formed the valley's northern side. Wide steps led to it and in its midst sat one single polished boulder as tall as two men and as wide again.

136

In its center was a door, and in the open doorway there stood a man and woman taller than the others and seeming both ancient and ageless. They were raven-haired and clad in gray robes shimmering blue and rose as the dove's neck will. A single green stone on a gold chain hung on the Lord's breast, and the Lady wore a chaplet of wood anemones, daisies, and violets. The gaze that they bent upon Eilian was curiously, gently bitter, and yet kind. It was as if they had expected her but mourned her coming.

"Child, I am Witonos, and this is my Lady, Wintida. How do you call yourself?"

"Eilian, if it please you, sir." Her voice was very small, and it trembled.

"Eilian. So be it." He looked at her gravely and then nodded, as if imparting some message to the company gathered below the steps where he stood. With a sigh like the wind, they turned and disappeared among the mounds.

Goronwy put an arm around Eilian. Anger darkened his face, but he held his tongue, sensing more than he understood.

Wintida, seeing the gesture, came down the stair to offer her hand. "Do not mistake us, Eilian. Though your coming be unwelcome, it is accomplished; and therefore we make you welcome despite all else."

She drew Eilian up the stair and Goronwy after. With Witonos leading, they passed through the wide portal into the hill.

Beyond the great doors lay an anteroom hung with tapestries and seemingly unfinished, for the rock was clearly living rock, roughly hewn. Yet, as they came into the great hall beyond, Eilian saw that this was not so. Like the carvers of the river boat and of Túdual's house, the shapers of stone had left the beauty of the rock to speak for itself, only smoothing here to heighten the movement of a line or pattern, or chipping there to show the gleam of crystal. Even a wide vein of slate became a riffled pattern echoed in the paving of the broad floor.

In the midst of the hall, a small fire licked and purred cozily on a low circular hearth below the high dais. Witonos and Wintida moved up to the two high-backed oaken chairs overlooking the hearth and motioned the children to sit on the rim of the fire circle, facing them. As Eilian's eyes became accustomed to the flickering light, she saw that another company stood around the walls. Unlike the folk outside, they went cloaked and hooded.

"Do you know why you have come, Song-Child?"

These folk, like Goronwy, seemed overfond of riddling. Why was this a puzzle?

"Because my uncle was hurt, and I was brought?"

Witonos waved an impatient hand. "No, no. Beyond that. Have you no old tale among your people, your own blood, of vengeance you owe those of the Fair Family known as the Children, the *Plant Rhys Dwfn?*"

"N-no. None that I have heard." She held fast to Goronwy's hand, for the Lord Witonos's questions were echoed in the tension of the watchers around the walls, and she was frightened despite her determination not to shame her friend.

"She could not know." An old man, shorter and bearded, but very much like Túdual, stepped into the circle of firelight. "It is an old tale among the Children and therefore ages past remembering for mortal men. Nothing would remain for them but unrest at the unrecalled, drawing the descendants of the Singer to us—to their doom and ours— across the span of long ages. Why else were those who dared call themselves Red Fairies drawn together at last? Why in their wandering did they come in the end to camp upon our borders? Oh, I am sure they thought it chance, but they could not escape it."

Eilian, understanding only this last, was awed. She looked first to Goronwy, and then toward Witonos the king.

"It is true. They thought it was my grandfather holding them here. Emrys says when he died, they thought to go wandering again. And could not."

Witonos nodded thoughtfully. He seemed deeply weary, and to Eilian, though his eyes seemed silver in the fire's light, he was not so terrible as old wives' tales would have him. "Aye," he said. "And our worry these last years grew to certainty. We tried often to be rid of them, always taking care not to show ourselves. We loosed ponies, broke down pens, and made paths seem to turn back upon themselves. Yet, though they came to fear the wood, they stayed."

He turned to the old man. "Garym, I have sent watchers to their dingle, but from what the lad here has told us, we must set a wider watch. This, too, my people can do, but it is too dangerous for us to venture into Trawsfynydd or Llanfachrueth. Our faces, our eyes betray us, and after yesterday's work your folk are no safer. But you—with your white hair and beard—in suitable clothing you could pass for an aged *cerddor*, a wandering poet, could you not? And an ear well tuned in the alehouse nearest Perllan would not be amiss."

The old man smiled. "Aye, my lord. If we have a harp that will not betray us. My own is of *findruin* metal and ashwood carved with runes."

"Come then." Witonos rose and drew the old man aside to speak with him in the shadows. The Lady Wintida beckoned Eilian to sit at her feet and bade Goronwy leave if he wished. He stayed but drew back into the shadows, wondering.

Wintida smiled. "I think your Goronwy has told you little, despite his small discretion. You know that we are a folk whose generation spans long ages, to whom the duration of a mortal man seems but the falling of a leaf, and you are thinking that you would wish to remain here with us. But could you bear to see us unfading while you dwindle to your death?"

She had not thought of that. And did it mean that Goronwy was ages old while still a boy?

" 'Change-child!' " the lady murmured. "Oh, I will not say we have not stolen children, but it would be nearer truth to say they fled to us and regretted it too late. And what does 'change' mean to you, child?"

"Why—change . . ." She hesitated to speak before so many. "Why, to—to not care for my lameness, to have skill in the four and twenty measures of poetry. To have beauty all around, as you have. And . . ." Her voice fell. "To be free of hurts."

She looked up to see compassion in the Lady Wintida's eyes.

"Change is then a sort of magic? A line you step across? A wand I wave? Ah, what I could have accomplished with a wand!" She laughed ruefully. "But then, if change were so lacking in reason, all our misgivings should turn to fears and our regrets to despair."

Eilian was muddled. "Change is not good then?" she ventured, doubtfully.

"On the contrary, child. All that is good comes through it. But it is no sudden shift played *on* you. It must be planted and tended *in* you, for what is growth but change and transformation? To fear it is to invite decay, but to live in hope it be imposed upon you by some kindly fate is to live a fool."

"I do not understand. Am I so foolish?" No sooner had

she said it than a thought brushed past Eilian of the aching sameness, the dreaming-of-when-things-would-be-different-ness, of so many of her days.

The Lady smiled. "Only in thinking we can give you love and peace if you have not tended the seeds of these things in your own heart. This is the Last Garden, not the First. It is a refuge, not a kingdom. A pleasant prison for those of us who have found we cannot live with men, but would not leave this green and growing Middle Earth." She stroked Eilian's fair hair. "Come, you must listen to a tale the Lady Rhelemon has to tell."

A woman stepped out of the shadows. She wore a gown like dull silver, but her hair held all the silver sheen the robe lacked. She wore it braided and twisted in a coronet, fastened by a pin set with a green stone.

"I am Rhelemon, my dear, sister to the lords Túdual and Garym." She spoke in a slow, rich voice, oddly high and clear. "We are the eldest of those known as the Children, the Children of Rhys the Cunning. Our blood is not that of the Gwyllion, Witonos's folk, though we have long been allied with them and our tales remember the world's green morning as do theirs. Yet the tale Wintida speaks of is another. It concerns a mortal man. The Children knew him by no name but the Singer, and his voice was as sweet as the nightingales of Logres and as rich as all the valleys of Gwales. A lame man, dark and young, he came among us where we lived above the place later men called Betws-y-Coed. He was made welcome, for we could not withstand his singing, all sweetness and pain commingled. Our lord in that age was Aderyn, and he and his long-beloved, the Lady Ywen, gave the Singer food and raiment and begged that he would stay. At first he remained for kindness' sake, and then for pleasure's. But all did not go well, and in time he left—secretly—taking the beautiful Ywen with him, for she would not be parted from his gentleness and the sweetness of his music." Rhelemon sighed. "The Lord Aderyn raged and cried of the daggers in his heart and fell into a strange illness. Afterward he wandered in a beggar's guise until he found them. The tale is too much to tell, but briefly, he slew the Singer and laid a curse upon the offspring Ywen had borne him—that they should be wanderers in Middle Earth and not know peace. Poor Ywen in her fury answered with another curse. One day one born of her own and the Singer's blood should see the Children driven out from Middle Earth."

As Rhelemon spoke, the way she uttered "the Singer" seemed to Eilian directed at her. At the tale's end she saw Goronwy move into the firelight as if to protest, taller and stronger in his anger, and his gray eyes for the first time as frightening, as silver, as Witonos's own.

Witonos had returned without Garym.

"Hold your tongue, boy," he warned. "What is, is. And a tale may hold more than this surface meaning that we fear. Come, we must let the child herself see what it is you are dreading."

He gestured, and lamps were lit in brackets around the walls. Those thirty or more who had watched and listened silently pushed back their hoods and dropped their cloaks to the floor.

Their eyes were blue, and their hair gleamed the fairest of red-gold.

143

TEN

"Oh, I could manage a carol perhaps. Something in praise of a maid who's soft as a butterfly with green and blue wings." Emrys laughed, looking at Pilipala in her green gown.

"Do you know *none* of the measures, then?"

"Look you, Eilian. I am a harpist of sorts, not a poet. The harp has but so many strings and so many notes you can coax from them, but even there there's more to the art than knowing so. Myself, I hear a song and I can play it. No more. As for poetry, a low-born harper is not invited to sit at the *pencerdd*'s feet to study measures. How should I know them?"

They sat in the ash grove below Túdual's house, where cushions and rugs had been spread under the trees and a basket of luncheon provided. While Emrys ran his fingers along the wood of the harp and plucked a string or two, Pilipala was busied making flower chains, and Túdual wandered along the stream, an eye cocked for herbs. Eilian sat leaning against a standing stone.

Goronwy refilled his cup. "Your fingers move surely on

the harp strings. As deftly almost as Garym's. Are all your tunes then 'heard' ones?"

"No, not all," Emrys admitted, wiping his mouth with the back of his hand. "But they've no words to go with, those others."

"I could teach you some of the measures," said Eilian eagerly. "And then you could make songs and bend the tunes to fit them."

"Aye, I meant to ask you that," said Goronwy, raising an eyebrow at a slice of bread before taking a bite of it. "Where ever did you learn the shaping of an *englyn?*"

"From the parson at Caerhûn. He has them writ in a secret book to study, and let me copy out the simpler ones."

Goronwy choked on the crust of his bread, and Emrys snorted with amusement, holding down the laugh for fear of the pain in his chest.

"And if *I* could read, I could be a poet and join the guild of bards? Oh, sweet child, a scratch on paper is only a poor echo of a shape and sound! It takes a long time and well-tuned ears to be learning such a craft."

Eilian was distressed. She turned to Goronwy. "Why . . . have I been making such shapeless songs, then?"

"More so since you came from the North than before," Goronwy said, but kindly. "Think of your changeling song, this last one. Oh, it was full of your feeling, but to the listener it was all the voice that wove the spell. The words fell into nonsense without measure or *cynghanedd*. I think there is no sound as sweet as your singing. But your songs? We-e-el, perhaps when you are growing gray . . ."

"Oh, you are spiteful!" She slapped at him and missed. "What do you know of *cynghanedd* or of rhyming?"

"What would you have? Cross-alliteration, balanced and unaccented?" He swept his arm in a wide gesture toward Emrys and the distant Túdual.

"Harpist playing, herbalist plucking.

"Or would you have *cynghanedd draws?*" He bowed to Pilipala and to herself, proposing:

"Trysting stones and maidens trusting.

146

"Some are as difficult as any poet could wish. For *cynghanedd groes o gysswllt*, you must begin the repetition of consonants before the main pause instead of after. There, Eilian! A book would tell you as much as that. Can you make a verse which does so?"

"Hai! No, give me time." She clapped her hands to her head. "Drato! It isn't fair to spring it on me so." She screwed her eyes shut and at last ventured:

"Nettles open, turtles appear?"

Pilipala giggled. Emrys tilted his head back and after a bit of thought offered:

"Daystars bend, asters bloom."

"Aye, better, better," Goronwy applauded. "But for our matchless nightingale, I would offer a modest couplet of *cynghanedd lusg*:

"Love, bring to your sweet singing—"

Emrys' ear caught at the pattern, and he finished it triumphantly:

"More time spent on the rhyming!"

"Now the both of you are being spiteful." Eilian protested but, to her own surprise, was relieved—even oddly pleased. Before she could ponder that to understand it, Goronwy turned to Emrys, pressing him to play.

"But, such a splendid harp it is. My rough songs are not fit for its strings. And I know few others. Is the harp your own?"

"Hardly that." Goronwy laughed. "No, it is the Lord

Garym's. He has taken my shabby one a-spying with him and left me the use of this beauty."

Emrys handled it lovingly. "It could be Teirtu's magical harp, it is so fine." He gently plucked a three-fingered chord. "Niece, do you know the old lay of the Drowned Lands?"

"Yes, yes. Mam taught it me long ago, but I can remember it every word. My tongue needn't limp over the choosing of phrases," she quipped.

Twined together, the harping and the song winged through the wood, the measure true and descant sweet. Eilian sang of the waters loosed upon the kingdoms of Teithi Hen, Helig ap Glannawg, and of Rhedfoe ap Rheged, of the loves lost, and the towers and steeples travelers still saw beneath the waters. The harping, mean and treble and sweet chords, moved, soared, cresting at last in the swirl of the waters and in the dim ring of bells beneath the sea.

Pilipala's flowers lay forgotten in her lap. Túdual, drawn from his herb-gathering, stood amazed, looking down at his patient.

"And you a mortal man! Can many mortals sing and play as you two? It was not so in my days out in the wider world."

Emrys leaned back against the tree, wearied by the excitement of the playing. "I have never held such a harp. It *is* the magic harp of Teirtu!"

"No," said Goronwy. "Even my father would be hard put to outdo you. A second Sion Eos you are!"

"Only here, with the singer and the song and this." Emrys caressed the harp. "My own harp has a bitter edge to

148

its music. My own harp." He repeated the words half to himself, and with a wry smile. "There was once a plaque at its base to tell how its owner had won it in '94 at the Eisteddfod. He did not have it long. And my father beat me when I came back with it instead of the cow he sent me to steal. A second Sion Eos, you say? Like as not I will be ending with the hangman as he did."

Túdual heaved a great sigh. "It is a bitter path your folk have followed. And who is to say the root of it is in Aderyn's curse? To my mind it lies more in the Singer's act, for he made another's love his own. And acts beget acts. Still, there's a deceitful ease in judging simply. Earth belongs to all who walk upon her, and in this business of 'mine' and 'thine,' we must go gently and with humor at our foolishness. To die for thieving? The remedy is worse than the act. But if men's laws and our own are imperfect, there is another law that is not, for all its risk. Earth herself brings forth, man grows, the seed becomes a fruit tree with his tending and will bear. He is himself a creature meant to grow and to tend, and each has some fruit worth bearing. My son, what business had you, with an ear for all the shades of sound and a mind that must dance in numbers— what business had you to be a thief? That is to be—to be as the fluted fungus living on the beech, or the rust that withers wheat, or the mistletoe as it stifles the branch's life. Oh, some of these are lovely, tempting things, but they live on loss and death and are the agents of decay." His anguish was real, for he had come to be fond of his charge.

It was Pilipala who answered softly, unexpectedly. "Aye, we have lived on the knife's edge and not known how sharp it was until Eilian's coming."

Emrys looked at her, smiling. "But not you. You have never taken what was not your own. You fed and served and tended in a fruitless orchard."

"But I ate, too, and killed the chickens and geese for the roasting," she said, distressed that he should think of her as other than himself.

Túdual cleared his throat, unhappy at the turn he had given to their talk. Goronwy took the harp again and struck a riffle of notes as if to lift the company out of the somber mood it had fallen into. But no song followed, for the sound of horns broke across the valley's peace.

"The sentinels. Something is amiss." Goronwy propped the harp against a tree and stood, alert and unmoving, his eyes closed as if that sharpened his hearing. "A rider is coming through the pass," he said. "And fast. The ferry goes to meet him."

He turned to the others, who could hear nothing but the ringing of horns as some alarm was passed along the road north to Castell Witonos. There was silence and then, ringing back from the northern cliff, an answering horn.

"Something strange is up," he said. "I'll be back directly."

Rather than go around by the bridge, he leaped the stream and disappeared in the direction of the orchard and the river meadows.

"Won't the cousins have heard the horns?" said Eilian fearfully.

"No." Túdual spoke absentmindedly, staring thoughtfully in the direction of the pass. "From the peaks above the river to the northern wall, the valley is much like a great cup. Though sounds ring clearly here, they do not spill over. And if they did, the Great Wood would swallow them. I cannot think what the trouble is unless some one of your kinsmen has wandered too far this way. We have had no report from my brother Garym of trouble brewing."

Before long Goronwy had returned, running as lightly as before.

"I came to the crossroads a moment too late. The messenger had passed already, mounted on a fresh pony. Those at the ferry said that he came from the watchman farthest south along the river, with some word about an encampment on the wood's edge and a company of men marching up the South Road to the fording place. Something big's afoot."

"The dingle!" Emrys struggled to raise himself. "The Squire must mean to root my people out. They must be warned."

Túdual protested, soothing him. "They shall be. If their own watchers have not already seen, ours will contrive somehow to raise an alarm. Even if you were fit to ride, you would come too late."

"Beside which," Goronwy added, "once the horns have sounded, no one departs the valley without the Lord's permission."

"It is because of me again," Eilian said. "I will go to Lord Witonos to ask a pony and leave to go. If everything began with my coming, it can end with my going. Can't it?" She was pale and earnest.

"To Perllan? No!" Goronwy's protest was echoed by the others.

"I don't like the idea much myself," said Eilian, more calmly than she felt. "But what if *those* men stumbled too far into the wood?"

"You do not mend a sleeve by unraveling it," said Goronwy, in distress.

Túdual held up a hand to quell their argument. "It does no good to wrangle here. We must go to Castell Witonos. The danger may not be so great after all. Eilian child, Goronwy will fetch you a pony so that the two of you may go ahead of us. And Goronwy, send someone to the barns to fetch the apple wagon to me. Pilipala and I will ride in it with Emrys. Go! Get you gone!"

It seemed the whole of the valley had gathered within the half-moon of trees that stood before Castell Witonos. A herald sounded his horn, and Witonos himself came out through the portal of the fortress, as if he meant to address the quiet, waiting company. Yet, seeing Eilian, he stopped and made a sign, so that the crowd opened to let the ponies pass. Dismounted, she and Goronwy were taken up the broad steps and through the wide doors. There in the homely outer room, they sat waiting in the carved and cushioned chairs that stood by the doors to the great hall. Then Witonos was with them, sweeping them before him, through the hall and into a smaller chamber where Wintida and the Lady Rhelemon sat waiting.

"There are men encamped upon the southern slopes, and they have sent scouts into the eastern and western foothills. The Red Fairies, as they presumed to call themselves, are scattered on the winds before them, but these men are not yet aware their quarry's fled. They have set to felling the trees along the southern rim. Do they think to drive the thieves before them as rabbits before the reaper? It makes no sense. Where *is* Garym? He should have given us forewarning of all this."

Witonos filled the room, a swelling energy that crossed and recrossed its tessellated floor. The tapestries along the walls sprang alive with his passing—scenes of unicorn hunts and strange landscapes with even stranger palaces and cities far richer than gently crumbling Conwy Castle or Caernarvon had been even in the days when all their pinnacles and turrets still bore pointed roofs and bright pennants. It seemed to Eilian as if under the sense of violence in Witonos's tight-reined impatience an older world was summoned close, to shimmer under its picturing along the walls. She looked away and tried to think of other things. She was glad to hear that the cousins had fled. There was no need then to offer to go out from the wood as ransom for them. She was almost as much relieved not to have to face and speak with Witonos. In his pacing there was a leashed and straining power, in his grim face a radiance that threw all else within the room into shadow, making it a dark island in a world of harsh and stunning beauty. But the landscapes lurking behind the tapestries were no more alien than his shining face and silver eyes. Eilian turned to Goronwy, then hesitated. He was a kinsman of some sort to Witonos, after all. Goronwy was no fixed star upon the sphere that marked the bounds of her attention. More, he was his own person, and who knew what that was? "I want to go home," she thought. "Oh, please, I want to go home so very much. And sing, and manage the dairy, and take the lambs to market."

Túdual and his charges came up the North Road at a gallop, carrying a disheveled and still breathless Garym with them in the apple wagon. They were accompanied into the great hall by the elders of those living in the valley who

153

were, like the Children, branches of the Fair Family, the Ellyllon. Witonos and the others came from the smaller chamber to meet them.

"Lord of the Gwyllion," Garym said, "it has come." He tried to recover some measure of dignity, but in his bristling beard, his beggar-minstrel garb, and near-exhaustion he did not waste words on the formalities of greeting. "Soldiers—longbow men—marched eastward out from Harlech two days past, and the word in the alehouses is that Sir Edmund Rastall's men are furnished with pikes and axes, and others ride north from his great house in Cardiganshire. I could not come by road. Rumor has a Justice of the Peace at every crossroads, and their Overseers have conscripted farmers armed with axes. The fording places are guarded, too, so I needs must go over the hills like a goat and creep down from the west. They have riders on the foothills, but I have not lost all my craft."

"This much we know in part," said Witonos impatiently. "But *why?* And why do you come so late and riding from the east, so Relynos says, in a wagon?"

"There, my lord, I misjudged. Yet I cannot think the outcome all ill. It was young Eilian's folk they hungered after, and since I was fitly dressed and would not therefore frighten them further, I rode by way of the dingle to give them warning. Yestereve this was. And they took flight as soon as the moon was up." He scratched his head, looking oddly human and abashed. "Their ponies all were wandered off, and so I gave 'em mine for the old woman to ride and saw them as far as the paths that scatter to the east. If I have been overlong in coming, it is because from early morning there were men abroad in the wood. I had a bit of a

154

scramble, coming down at last by the brook that joins the eastern river near my brother's house."

"Perhaps they will go away." Eilian was as startled as the others to hear herself speak out. She felt very small and shy to dare address such a council. "When they find the dingle empty, I mean. And if they do not—why, I must go out to them. I would rather wed Simon Rastall than . . . "

"No, child, no." Garym interrupted her. "There is no way out in that direction, for why do you think Sir Edmund rages like a bullock in torment, to fling these forces against the wood?"

The hall was silent. Even Witonos spoke no word or question. Only Pilipala moved, pressing her hands over her mouth as if to deny its answering.

"I heard it in the alehouse south of Perllan," Garym said. "Sir Edmund's son is dead. Of the old woman's curse, Rastall thinks. It was on his returning from the encounter by the ford, while her words still rang in his companions' ears. His horse stepped in a hole, in sight of the windows of Perllan, and the boy was taken to his father, dead of a broken neck. For that his father swears to cut the wood down, tree and seedling—all of it—so thieves will never shelter in it again."

Witonos rose slowly from his seat. "Then we must take up arms," he said. His wrath filled the great hall like the beating of dark wings upon the air, and his countenance was like a lamp at last unshaded, fair but perilous. Eilian saw for the first time that he already bore a sword at his side, long and broad-bladed. He exulted.

"If they come beyond the pine woods, they will pay a man for every tree. But doubt not, once they see us and know us for what we are, they will not rest until we are destroyed. And the race of men are like the sands along the sea. Yet though our power has dimmed, though Aradnos and Hafgan and Gwynn ap Nudd are gone from Middle Earth into the Other Kingdoms, this shall prove a battle no less worth the singing than the Three Wars of the Fortresses, whether any be left behind to sing it or no."

Eilian drew close to Emrys and Pilipala as Witonos led the elders out to the portal and the broad steps to face the Tylwyth Teg. They were terrible. Beautiful enough to break your heart with the watching; terrible, for it was a searing, white-faced beauty like the center of the candle-flame that, watched too long, flares against the eyelids long hours after. Only Goronwy among them held back, shining and yet torn.

The crowd heard Witonos's ringing words with mingled passion and despair, but the tongue he spoke was strange to Eilian: rich, with a sound of wind and water. Then he turned to those behind him.

"In the Elder days we might have sent you out to our enemies. But Garym's impulse to warn your kin was right, and you shall be served as fairly. For, however thinly, Ywen's blood is in you, and we will not pay you for our doom. Goronwy, kinsman! You know the trail that passes overhead. Take ponies—those Durwen holds will do—and see these three come home at last. And give your father greeting. When I am slain, he in his hut shall be king."

There was no breathing space for argument. The ponies were brought, and Eilian, riding in a daze, found herself following fourth and last a narrow track beside a small stream that tumbled down the hills to spill out near the cliff face and Castell Witonos.

Some fifty yards of climbing and the path turned back from the waterway, for from that point its bed rose too steeply, the brook spilling down in a falling, frothing ribbon. The trail doubled back above itself, cutting sheer across the cliff's face. Eilian could not bear to look. The ledge was no more than three feet wide, if that. It climbed across the rock wall and, with difficult and awful turnings, bent back to climb the other way, scaling the mountainside in stages. After what seemed an age, her pony stopped, and she opened her eyes to find the others halted, too, while Goronwy gingerly dismounted and edged back to steady Emrys with one hand. Emrys' pony had stopped when she felt her rider sway dizzily.

"It will pass," Emrys mumbled. "A moment or two, that's all. Lightheaded."

Winding her fingers more tightly in her pony's mane, Eilian looked down. Some faces were upturned to watch their progress, but most of those gathered before Castell Witonos had turned to watch two green-clad archers who came riding along the North Road where it passed among the mounds. Sentinels of the wood, Eilian guessed, and she wondered that they should have left their posts.

The four were too high to hear what was reported, but saw that for a moment the host of y Tylwyth Teg did not believe it. And then they stirred and scattered, running to the mounds, the Children to their houses. Some who were already mounted turned toward the steep stream and came quickly up behind Goronwy and his charges.

"What is it?" Goronwy called.

The raven-haired maid who rode in front pointed. "We cannot war with that," she said.

Above the orchard and the meadows, sweeping around the valley's sides the way the wind went, was a thin haze of smoke. And beyond the peaks that guarded the river pass, green fir trees burned like candles in the afternoon.

In an hour's time the Last Garden was emptied, its people moving across the northern hills. Some clutched at burdens and would not look back to see the great black cloud that lowered over the flaming wood, though it was not the first time men had driven them from long-loved homes. Witonos and Wintida came last. When they were safely off the uppermost reach of the narrow trail, past the standing stone that marked its head, Witonos turned to raise his hand in a gesture that was at once command and farewell. Awed, Eilian and the others saw the great stone vanish. There was a rumbling and a great cloud of dust that was the passing of Castell Witonos. The fire would destroy all else that could betray them.

With Goronwy, Emrys, and Pilipala, Eilian rode north. The others passed like a wind into the east and were gone.

ELEVEN

Mam sat by the window, stitching at a piece of crewel-work. "You have more embroidery in your head, girl, than's ever come from my needle onto cloth," she said. "Oh, I don't discount *all* you say. There's Emrys vows it's so. But he was fevered from his hurts and apt to be seeing oddities. Drato!" She sucked a pricked finger. "It is growing too dim to be working."

"Shall I light a candle, Mam?"

"No. Only on Midsummer Eve could I be working so late as this, as it is. I will put it away until tomorrow. A candle! Here we are in a grand house, and I must be pinching pennies and grudging candle ends."

Dad roused from his dozing. "Aye, my girl," he rumbled. "And I'll hear no more of seeing the moneylender again. We've come to Plaseirian too late to clear neglected land and plant, and too early to be affording more lambs. Llwyn Cerddin and our sheep have two families to keep now."

Mam shook her head, wondering. "To see my baby brother wed! If only the girl did not wear such peculiar clothes . . ."

Eilian laughed. She had had to roll her own green dress and blue petticoat up and hide them under a floorboard in her bedroom for fear Mam would try to burn them. Mam called it a "nasty elvish thing" and said it made her come cold all over.

"Well may you laugh," said Mam, "but I was *sure* the poor old parson would refuse to read out the banns, he was so distracted by the outlandish look of the both of them."

Dad stood to stretch. "Shall I send another of the young ewes back to Llwyn Cerddin so that your brother may sell it to buy cloth for breeches and a gown for his bride?"

"No," Mam exclaimed in some alarm. "They very well can wait until the flax in the bottom field comes ready."

"I will have to be teaching Pilipala how to spin the linen thread, and weave, and how to milk a cow," Eilian said.

Mam, following the train of her own thought, went on. "If you are of a mind to sell a sheep, sir, we are more in want of candles, and glass for mending cracked windows, than Emrys is of breeches." She stopped. "*Cow?* What cow would she be milking?"

"Ah, Mam, I do love you!"

An astonished Mam found herself wrapped in a tight, warm hug. She was too sharp not to know that it had something to do with her unconvincing and grudging swing from extravagance to cheeseparing, but could not take offense. She was too shaken by the warmth, the touching, from this one among her daughters whom she had feared for her looks that were an echo of the unhappy past. Eilian, for her part, found it surprisingly easy to love her mother, though never in the world could she have managed to say straight out, "You are you and—how strange it is—I wish you no different!"

"Away with you, Eilian. You are grown too old to sit in my lap." Mam smoothed her apron tidily, but there were red spots on her cheeks for pleasure. Looking up, she eyed Dad. "*What* cow?"

He tapped his cold pipe out in the fireplace, avoiding her accusing glance. "Um. Well, Alis's daughter. By way of a bit of dowry, seeing the girl had no father to send bride gifts with her." He began carefully refilling the pipe.

"No more did *I*," Mam said. "And no one gave *us* a cow to set up housekeeping with. Emrys might as well have had a proper dowry, I am thinking, for what he has had from you already. And though our Eilian says he can harp the birds from the trees, Ifan Roberts, you cannot be knowing if he can farm. Llwyn Cerddin needed a tenant, yes. But a frugal and responsible one. Like Twm Williams."

"Twm *Williams!* Aye, so frugal he would sell the manure rather than be spreading it on the ground. Out of one pocket into another. *There's* economy for you. No, Emrys is a good lad. He will learn."

Mam made a grudging sound of assent. "Aye, now Mamgu is heard of, going about with Elis, doctoring and selling herbs. If she dares turn up here after all she's done, I hope it is later than sooner, so that Emrys can have the house too full of children to keep her. Of course," she added glumly, "*we* have a surfeit of rooms. All but empty of furniture as well," she added, shifting back to more immediate preoccupations. "Little did I think, when Attorney Llewellyn sent for you from Ludlow and you came riding home t'other week with Plaseirian in your hand, that I should come here in my old gown and not a penny for an oaken dresser and the small tables I've been wanting."

"All in time, girl. All in time." Dad lit a taper in the small fire that he kept burning every day "to cure the damp," and held it to the pipe's bowl, sucking carefully.

Mam folded her work and put it on the table. "So you have said all this week. Hai, I am off to bed now. Do not be long. And do not wake the little ones by treading on the loose stair."

When she had gone, Eilian, not in the least sleepy, said, "May I see the paper, Dad? The one you brought from the great lords at the Council?"

"Now? No, tomorrow when there's light enough to see it by, sweet. It is only a copy the Clerk's deputy made for me, but it has the Council's seal to say we may have Plaseirian without waiting the pleasure of the Sessions, as it is clear what their judgment must be. It is full of lawyers' words to pad it out, but in among them it says that the defendant, Sir Edmund Rastall, appeared only after the sheriffs of Merioneth and Cardiganshire were ordered to proclaim for his appearance."

"And did he truly offer no defense against your claim?"

"Not a word. It was as if the faster he were rid of Plaseirian and us, the better. He spoke no word to me. And some were telling today in Conwy that he has sold his other lands in Wales and gone to England." He drew her close to his chair. "You have come home to us fatter and sweeter, child. You begin to be a woman. But what has happened to the poetess, whose great fame was to stretch out across the Marches?"

"I've thought and thought about that, Dad. The poetess . . . she thought she had only the singing, you see. I suppose she thought you loved her because you were soft, for *she* saw nothing lovesome in her. Yet even Mam would love

162

an important Personage, and so I thought to become one." She laughed. "Oh, I was so green!"

Dad looked at her with amusement. "And now you are golden in your wisdom? Come, you are not going to be giving up the making of songs? Perhaps your muse was a bit halting, but that seems chopping down the apple tree because it is not bearing cherries!"

"No, I do love the making. But as Emrys and Goronwy have delighted in telling me, I've not the head for weaving intricate patterns and trimming my pictures of words to fit the measure's frame. I shall sing my untidy bits and pieces, too, but mostly I would like to learn the old songs—and Emrys', if he becomes a proper poet."

"It sounds good to me. And you *shall* have the dairy to manage. I will be buying new heifers next year, and I take Alis tomorrow to Rowli Jones's bull to get another calf. With luck, it will be a bull calf. We will not be missing the young cow that goes to Emrys. Come, let us close the house up and get us to bed." He moved to the fireplace, knocked out his pipe again, and scattered the ashes of the fire with his boot.

Eilian closed the narrow windows and fastened the shutters. "When did you take up smoking tobacco stuff, Dad? You never had a pipe before."

"Eh? Oh, in Ludlow, I think it was. Yes, in Ludlow. The gentlemen at the inn there always sat down to a tankard and a pipe of an evening, and I thought it very pleasant."

She came beside him to the bottom of the stair and pinched him teasingly. "And Mam with no candles to her table?" she asked in a mournful voice.

He snorted, trying to hold back his deep laugh. "Oh, she

shall have her candles and a bit more, little Eilian. Thanks to their lordships in Ludlow awarding me costs, the money I laid out for Clerk's fees and the like is back in my own pocket now. If it were not, I should go to the moneylender after all, for Plaseirian will pay us soon enough. We need not scrimp so very tightly. Come along. Up you go!"

Coming behind her, he thought that she no longer limped so painfully, but put it down to his imagination. "Still," he thought, "it is the *real* child's come home."

Eilian's bed, for the time being, was bundles of rushes tied together, but it was freshly made up with linen sheets and a fine light blanket, all Mam's handiwork. Once a week a clean white nightdress lay folded on top. The idea of special clothes to go to bed in, and having to bathe sometimes even more than once a week, was amazing and delicious. Her pleasure at the fresh things was forgotten, though, when she moved to the window to look out on the hillside and down to the glimpse of the broad silver River Conwy gleaming between two hills. Late as it was, the midsummer evening lingered, only reluctantly giving way to the darkness behind the eastern hills. Moving to the south window, she knelt and rested her arms on the ledge, to watch the dusk beyond the elm tree growing in the tangled, overgrown roses by the gate into the lane. A last lamp winked out in the shadow that was Roe Wen.

Somewhere at the near edge of that shadow, Emrys and Pilipala slept on a bed of rushes like her own, in Mam and Dad's old bedchamber. "Llwyn Cerddin is just there," she thought, puzzling out the distant yew tree and the line of witchens. Then, not with her eyes, nor ears, she heard or saw—somehow—and knew someone stood and called her. There followed a silver trill, a whistle, and somewhere a movement of stirring, of waking. Had those high sweet notes sounded in her mind or in her ear, she wondered. They drew her to her feet and to the other window, but there she heard the sound no more. Drawn by her tiredness and the sunny smell of the clean, rough linen, she sat on the bed but immediately felt restless. The feeling eased as she returned to the south window, yet it seemed as if a thread fastened below her heart thrummed with a sound below the edge of hearing, pulling at her. Without thinking, as if obeying, she opened the casement wide, pulled up the front of her skirt to tuck it in her waistband, and climbed feet-first through the window. Sitting on its ledge, she could just manage to reach a limb of the wide elm tree, to swing onto it and creep in toward the trunk, where she let herself down through the laddered branches. Out through the roses and the gate, she followed the shadowy ribbon of road toward Roe Wen, not knowing why.

She came into the village but did not go uphill toward Llwyn Cerddin, turning instead down through the sleeping handful of cottages beside the banks of the Roe. Somewhere there was the faint tinkle of a silver bell. At the crossroads beyond, she found Emrys before her, and Pilipala in her bare feet, rubbing one sleepy foot against the calf of her other leg.

"Eilian, is it? How can you have heard it, too?"

"Heard what?" The thread of unheard sound pulled at her again. She did not wait for an answer, but moved quickly and surely along the gray road that ribboned through a landscape invisible in the darkness. The others caught her up at the first bridge and, keeping pace, told how, sleeping, they had heard a whistle that could have been no other than Goronwy's to his pony.

"And there was a sad note to it," said Pilipala. "So for worrying, we came."

Eilian ran. Past the second bridge over the winding Roe, the road bent toward Caerhûn, where she slowed and they came up again.

"You have not turned the ankle, have you, Eilian?"

"No, Emrys, but it is telling me to treat it with more respect." She laughed breathlessly. "Look you, the moon is rising. I mean to make for the river. It is something to do with the river."

In the moonlight they came beyond Caerhûn along the turning to the grassy earthworks of Canovium, the ancient Roman fort. Inside its moon-filled square, a pony cropped the silver grass, and past the church, on the riverbank below, sat Goronwy. Coming together, they said no words, sensing that something beyond a fair evening had drawn the boy, as themselves, to the Conwy's edge. They sat in the grass and listened. Slowly, among the sounds of night, the crickets and the owl, there came a far-off golden harping down the valley, flowing above the river. Then—a long while after, it seemed—winding in a glittering line down the deepening channel, they saw coracles come, a splendid fleet, crowned with torches, whiter than seashells.

Larger far than the coracles of men, shell-shaped and shallow, each held four cloaked figures, with room for forty more. In the foremost the harper sat, fingering the winds and waters into sound, making the strings sing of trees and hills and all the loveliness of Middle Earth. The

166

coracles slid past, some fifty in all, and curving in a wide arc came to rest a little way below the watchers.

"It is the time of leaving," Goronwy said. "These are my father's folk. Word came from the east that we should make us boats and bring them down from the mountain lakes. Witonos has gathered our kindred from the eastern forests and rides this night to join us."

He led them along the shore toward the gleaming company and made them known to Riatros his father, and his mother Geleina. Riatros was tall and darkly fair, yet, though less forbidding than Lord Witonos, still distant in his manner. Geleina seemed more frail, though no less fair, and there was something like pity mixed with the love in the glance she turned on her son.

"Aye," she said. "Farewells are all the deathlier when they are to the hills of home and friends who come at the heart's call. If love did not command me go, I could as well remain here, remembering my good father and my mother's choosing."

Goronwy made no answer, and though his friends would have asked where and why the going, something in his bearing—a tension that a word might shatter into pain—kept them silent. Listening, they learned that the boats waited here for the high water that would carry them safely over the Arw rocks at the fourth hour of the morning. A command was given that the torches be doused, not for fear of men spying them, but so that Witonos's coming might be seen the better. "No man will meddle with us this night," said Riatros, "though many have seen us pass." They had come from the lakes and fastnesses of Eryri in answer to the command mysteriously borne to them, and at the appointed time.

No more had the last torch hissed out in the water than a wide swath of lights, a wind of diamonds, swept over the crest of hills across the river and down into the trees, to emerge again along the shore. After a moment's pause, a cluster of lights moved out onto the water, floating slowly across the Conwy some half mile or more below the waiting company.

"Why, they come by the ferry of Caven Gronaunt," Eilian whispered.

"The ferry keeper will be well paid," said Riatros, "though I warrant he is safely closed behind his shutters and content to stay so."

Only a little while and the riders came along the river meadow, Witonos and Wintida and other familiar figures. There was a strange elation in them all, as if each were sharpened, fined—almost, even, pitched at some height where deep sorrow and high joy were one. Back and forth the ferry plied until the third hour of the morning, and the silent company grew until it was as a host of stars gleaming on the grassy slopes. As each new group came, some riding and some afoot, the ponies were led to the ancient earth-work and bid stay, until they overflowed it and many were set to grazing in the fields beyond. The small treasures many carried were stowed in chests fastened one amidships in each boat. When all had come at last, Riatros plucked a single note, and Witonos addressed them in their own tongue, that strange and ancient music. Then, turning himself to Eilian, Emrys, and Pilipala where they stood, he touched their hands.

"Fare you well, my friends. I take my family where Aradnos and Hafgan and Gwynn ap Nudd and all our Elders have gone before us. If we have failed to live in good Middle Earth because we mingle ill with men, yet beyond the Winter Lights, at the moon's edge, we shall come to the apple gardens of ever-green islands where no winter blows. We shall come even to Tir na'nOg."

Wintida came beside him, and Rhelemon and Túdual with her.

"These we wish to give you for remembering by," she said, taking first a gift from the Children, a soft dove-gray cloak with the sheen of feathers, and draping it around Eilian's shoulders. "In this you may walk the evening hills unseen and sing the stars down close to listen." To Pilipala she gave a gown that shimmered like the moon caught in a silken web, together with a silver apple, a pretty toy for the children yet to come. For Emrys there were as many ponies as he wished to keep. The others would go wild upon the mountainsides.

There was little to say. The lights, the harps murmuring like golden honey, the perilous beauty of the host—it was all too like a dream from which one must awaken lest he drown. The Folk embarked, filling the boats, putting out the torches one by one, until only a single coracle clung near the shore.

"You must make your farewells, my son," said Riatros to Goronwy, who stood in the water midway between the boat and his friends on the bank.

"I—I have not known to whom I meant to say them."

His father sat immobile, holding so fast his harp that strings under the slender fingers snapped. He had feared just this for weeks, for Geleina's sake more than his own.

Goronwy stood straight and slim. "I cannot go. There is too much to lose."

"Rather you would lose Tir na'nOg and your Fair Family?"

Goronwy put a hand out to touch his father's. "But to pass unchanged from out among these homely things? To leave the winter far behind? And not see spring again, with all her lambs upon the hillsides? I cannot."

His father shook his head wonderingly, for these things, though pleasant, were not truly dear to him. "Would your coming then be so painful?"

"To Tir na'nOg? No, I am not such a fool, my father. Mortal men dream of it, too, for life is all summer there. But

I would be as the rooted shrub, plucked up before the berries come. And ripeness—is it not all?"

"So wise mortals say," answered Garym, whose coracle, laden with the Children, had drawn near. "And it is the blood of mortal men in you that says it." He held out his beautiful harp. "Take this then as gift. I lost your own somewhere near Perllan, and this may serve as payment and remembrance."

Riatros interrupted, anguished for his son. "But your choice is pain and death," he said.

Eilian limped out into the shallow water and slipped her hand in Goronwy's.

"No, my father," he said. "I choose time and change and the wonder of uncertainty. I would be a man."

His mother did not weep, but smiled. "My father was a good man, and happier than most. I understand, and wish you all the joy of your mortality."

"And passing is not forgetting," said Eilian softly.

Geleina kissed them both, and then the signal came of the water's fullness.

The great host drew cloaks about them and sat together, silver-eyed shadows in the white boats, while their oarsmen lifted broad paddles to dip them in the moon upon the waters. Slowly, they swung out and away, singing down the widening river, coming under the silent walls of Conwy Castle to the bay and west and northward to the sea, to move at last like whitecaps on the wide ocean beyond the realms of men.

EPILOGUE

Long after the boats were gone from sight, the change-children stood listening, joined together in a circle. And each Midsummer Eve after, they came to the shore below Caerhûn to watch the year bend again toward winter so that, out of it, spring might come. They sang it on its way, remembering. And in time children came with them, and grew, and went there in their stead when they could come no more. As late as Queen Anne's time, cottagers told of hearing singing from the river's edge too sweet almost to be from mortal tongues, and harping beyond the words to tell of it. And hearing, they fastened their shutters, for that bone-deep fear of otherness remains. Some say—though it may be wishful fancy—that singing still is heard. If that is so, the song has likely changed, for all things do in time; and even when it first was made, it held within it echoes of songs far older. For Eilian sang to her uncle's harping these words that Goronwy made:

"Where is Artair, and Gwenhwyfar
  Who were bright and fair as the rose,
    Alexander and Peredur,

Witonos, Owain, and all those,
Caesar with his eagle legions
And Roland holding back his foes?

"Yesterday, today, tomorrow—
Joy is bloom to time and sorrow.

"Where be they who were before us
Hawks on wrists and horses riding,
Who held these hills and fields;
Sweet maidens in their bowers biding,
Winding gold among their tresses,
Waiting knights long gone a-fighting?

"Yesterday, today, tomorrow—
Joy is bloom to time and sorrow.

"Where is their laughter and their song,
The life that all with games was spent?
Where the hawks and where the hounds,
Where the beauty youth had lent?
It is as if they never were,
Yet in our now their then is pent.

"Yesterday, today, tomorrow—
Joy is bloom to time and sorrow."

And then they made their way home, laughing and spinning tales of what the day had seen. Second had come home full of foxtails, with Spot barking and grinning behind. Pilipala had spilled the porridge in the fire, and Goronwy had sold four ponies at Caernarvon.

"And *I* have bought a cherry tree," said Eilian, "which I must plant tomorrow."

174